The Marrying Kind

The Marrying Kind

Monique Miller

URBAN
CHRISTIAN

www.urbanchristianonline.com

Urban Books, LLC
78 East Industry Court
Deer Park, NY 11729

The Marrying Kind Copyright © 2012 Monique Miller

ISBN 13: 978-1-60162-834-3
ISBN 10: 1-60162-834-X

First Printing June 2012
Printed in the United States of America

10 9 8 7 6 5 4 3 2 1

Distributed by Kensington Corp.
Submit Wholesale Orders to:
Kensington Publishing Corp.
C/O Penguin Group (USA) Inc.
Attention: Order Processing
405 Murray Hill Parkway
East Rutherford, NJ 07073-2316
Phone: 1-800-526-0275
Fax: 1-800-227-9604

The Marrying Kind

Acknowledgments

Thank you, Lord, for giving me the gift of writing. I love to be a wordsmith and bring characters to life. Thank you also to my Dad and Mom, William H. Miller & Ms. Gwendolyn F. Miller, for all of your love, encouragement and continued support. And a special thanks goes to my daughter, Meliah, for your daily encouragement that keeps me humble as you make me strive for the best so that I can be an example you can emulate.

Many thanks my sisters and brothers, Penny, Denita, Will, Christopher, and Christina. Keep on striving to meet your goals in life—love you all!

To Anthony, I know I've said it before and I'll say it again, thank you for your help, your encouragement, your fortitude, and caring during this process. Your assistance and impartation has been divinely on time. ☺

I cannot forget the WIC Chicks of Harnett County, NC. Thank you to: Annette, LaVonda, Beverly, Vickie, Sha'Keisha, Kerri, Jennifer, Carla, Monica and Mrs. Gaynelle, for helping with the cover and other technical stuff—like the apple Kool-Aid ☺ And I have not forgotten former WIC Chicks in Jacksonville, NC and Durham, NC—once a WIC Chick, always a WIC Chick.

There are quite a few author friends who I have to thank each time I write a book, because they have been tremendous blessings to me. So thank you Toschia, Jacquelin Thomas, Rhonda McKnight, Suzetta Perkins, Sherri Lewis, Stacy Hawkins Adams, and Tia Webster.

Keep on writing, ladies, and encouraging others as you have all encouraged me.

To my agent ShaShana Crichton, again I cannot thank you enough for your guidance and being my advocate. I am so glad you saw something special in my writing to take me as your client.

Thank you to Urban Books—Carl Weber. And thank you, Joylynn Jossel, for your patience during this whole process.

I want to especially thank the book fans, readers, book clubs, Facebook friends, and Twitter friends. Your support messages and postings continue to encourage me to build the fictional city of Silvermont, North Carolina with all of its inhabitants. And I am so glad that you want me to keep the books coming. **Thank you all for your continued support.**

Blessings!

Monique Miller
E-mail: authormoniquemiller@yahoo.com
Web site: www.authormoniquemiller.com

Chapter 1

Travis Wayne Highgate stood in front of the Family Dollar store and jingled the last bit of change he had in his pocket. He pulled the change out and counted it. It was exactly three dollars and twenty-seven cents. He shook his head thinking about the date he'd had a few nights before. He'd spent over fifty dollars on movie and dinner with a woman who, at the end of the night, didn't even have the decency to invite him into her house. She'd given him a peck on the cheek and said she'd call him the next day. Three days later, he still hadn't heard from her, she hadn't called, and didn't answer when he called her.

He pulled out his wallet to check again to see if he missed a ten or a twenty dollar bill. After searching through a couple of receipts he'd stuffed inside, he breathed a small sigh of relief when he found two dollars folded between the slips of paper. He could just kick himself for putting himself out there, letting another woman step on his outward showing of feelings. All he got at the end of the night was a peck on the cheek and empty pockets.

Travis knew if he was very frugal, he'd be able to find enough in the freezer section to last him for another day until his next unemployment check came in. After stepping aside to let a woman and her child exit the store, Travis strode through the door and headed straight for the freezer section. He pulled out a TV dinner, a bag of

Tater Tots, and a container with four Italian ices. Then he stepped over to one of the other food aisles and picked up a loaf of bread and a bottle of grape juice. Each of the items he'd picked up only cost a little over a dollar each. He already had peanut butter and jelly at the apartment.

He stepped into the line to pay for his items. As he waited, from the corner of his eye, he saw something float out of the hand of the woman standing in front of him. When Travis looked down he saw a crisp ten dollar bill lying just behind the woman's foot. He looked around to see if anyone else had noticed it. And for a split second he thought about covering the bill with his foot to retrieve it the first chance he got.

But then he thought better of it. Sometimes it felt like he had an angel and a devil sitting on his shoulders, with the devil trying to pull him in the wrong direction and the angel tugging him in the right direction. Today the angel was winning. Travis knew that nothing good came to those who did wrong.

He tapped the woman on the shoulder. "Excuse me, miss. You dropped some money."

The woman looked down and quickly picked up the ten. She clutched it in her hand. "Oh, my goodness," was all she said.

Travis said, "You're welcome," thinking the woman didn't have any manners.

The woman looked at him as if he were crazy and said, "Oh, thanks." Then she quickly averted her eyes.

Travis was perturbed by the woman's actions as she went on about her business, paying for her items and then leaving, never glancing back at him again.

"Wow," Travis said to himself. He couldn't believe the audacity of some women. It seemed like so many of them didn't have any home training, not like his ex-wife Beryl did. She would never have not called back after a date, or not said thank you to someone helping her out.

He took a deep breath. He and Beryl were over now and he had to come to grips with that. Life must go on. He started to think that maybe it would be better for him to cut all of his emotions off and just become a player.

Once at the register the total for Travis's items came up to five dollars and fifty-two cents. He felt as if the little devil on his shoulder had given him a little thump on his head for being so honest. He then eyed his selection and asked the cashier to hold on for a moment as he put the grape juice to the side and he returned to the food aisle, where he picked up a package of grape-flavored Kool-Aid instead. He thought he remembered having some sugar at the apartment. He purchased the items and then headed out.

His cell phone rang as he stepped outside of the store. He pulled it out and saw that it was Beryl. "Well speak of the devil. You sure do have perfect timing," he said under his breath. He pushed the end button to stop the phone from ringing and cut it off.

It was Beryl's fault that he was in this whole predicament in the first place. If only she had given him another chance. He shook his head and headed to the apartment. The closer he got to his place, Travis started feeling pretty good. In less than an hour he'd have a full stomach and even a little dessert to eat after his dinner. And to top that off, he even had a few cents left over from his purchase, enough to buy a cup of coffee the next morning at McDonald's.

But as soon as he reached his apartment door, his little bit of euphoria was deflated as he saw a folded note taped to the door with the numbers 256 printed in large black letters. He knew it wasn't anything from the post office or UPS; he hadn't ordered anything. There was a sinking feeling in his stomach with a strong inkling about the contents of the letter—an eviction notice.

He wasn't going to open the letter. He knew it would only spoil his appetite. He set the piece of paper on the kitchen counter and commenced fixing his dinner. Fifteen minutes later his food was ready, Kool-Aid and all. He pulled his TV tray in front of his secondhand recliner and popped a VCR tape into his VCR. After pressing play he sat down and started watching an episode of *The Biggest Loser*. It was one of his favorite reality shows. This episode was from a few seasons prior when he'd still had cable and was able to tape new shows.

After finishing his meal, Travis sat back in the chair to relax. And before he knew it, he was asleep. He awoke to someone knocking hard on his door. He wasn't expecting anyone and tiptoed over to the peephole to see who it was. And again his stomach felt just like it did when riding a rollercoaster at the point when it did a fast dip downward.

His landlord stood on the other side of the door, pacing impatiently. Then he pounded on the door sounding like he was using his fist. "Mr. Highgate. Mr. Highgate. If you are in there I need to talk to you about your rent." He paused as if waiting for an answer. "Mr. Highgate," the man said again. "Are you in there, Mr. Highgate? If you are, we need to talk about your rent payment."

The television was loud enough to be heard outside of the door, so the landlord probably knew he was at home. Travis wished the man would just go away. His heart beat furiously as he tried to stand stark still. He didn't want to take a step away from the door for fear that the floorboards might creak. So for what seemed like an eternity he stood peeking out of the peephole, taking shallow breaths. He hoped more than anything that the man wouldn't use his master key to open the door.

Then, after what seemed like an eternity of knocking and pounding, the man finally left. It was then that Travis remembered the note that had been taped to the door when he'd come home earlier.

He looked around for it and saw it sitting on the edge of the kitchen counter. After retrieving it he opened it up and saw that it was, in fact, an eviction notice. At the top was a red stamp that said "First Notice." According to the note, Travis had seven days to pay the late payment or he was going to be evicted. The late payment included that month's rent, as well as late fees and possible court costs if he was legally evicted.

His hands closed tight around the piece of paper. Then he moved over to the recliner and sat down hard as he tried to figure out just how he was going to pay the rent as well as the light bill and cell phone bill. Even though he was going to get an unemployment check that next day, it would still only cover just enough for the rent and late fees for the apartment. Just how was he supposed to see with no electricity, and how was he supposed stay in communication with the world if his cell phone wasn't working?

He shook his head wondering how he had gotten into this predicament in the first place. Then he remembered; it was all his Uncle Billy's fault. If it weren't for him, he wouldn't be in this particular mess of having to foot all the bills by himself.

Travis located his cell phone that he'd been charging and dialed his uncle's phone number from memory.

The call immediately went to the voice mail, and Travis hung up. He wasn't going to leave a message; he'd already left a couple of messages and Billy had failed to call him back. And if Travis didn't know any better, he'd think Uncle Billy was trying to avoid him. But Travis did know better. Uncle Billy was probably caught up with some girl, to whom he was professing his undying love. Whenever Uncle Billy hooked up with a woman, Travis was usually hard-pressed to find him.

He and his uncle had grown up together. They were only two years apart in age. Travis was now thirty-six years old. And the uncle part was something both of them joked about when they were old enough to understand families and relationships. As it turned out, Travis was actually two years older than his uncle. So while Travis called Billy Uncle, his uncle called him nephew Travis.

Looking at his watch, it was almost four in the afternoon. Billy got off work at five, and if Travis started walking right then he'd get to the job just before five and catch his uncle. He pocketed his cell phone, grabbed a jacket, and turned off the TV and VCR, then stepped back over to his peephole to see if the landlord might have reappeared.

Not seeing anyone through the peephole, Travis gingerly opened the door and looked out and saw another note taped to his door. Upon opening it, he saw the words "Second Notice" stamped in red at the top of the note. He wondered if it was legal for the apartment complex to put two notes on his door in one day. But after looking back at the first note, he saw that the dates on the letters were two days apart. The complex was obviously trying to cover itself, and how was he supposed to prove that he'd gotten the notes on the same day?

Travis knew it was just another way the system was trying to work against him. He threw both papers on the counter in the kitchen and left his apartment, headed to find his Uncle Billy. Hopefully his family member would come through for him and let him borrow a couple hundred dollars to help him get over until the next month.

Travis made it to his uncle's job with five minutes to spare. He looked up at the sky, which was forming dark gray clouds. A storm was approaching. This was truly a time when he wished he had a few extra bucks so he didn't have to walk. He hoped his uncle wasn't working late because he didn't want to have to stand out in the rain. Luckily, only a couple of minutes after five, Travis was relieved to see Billy sauntering out of the office building, laughing and chatting along with a couple of guys.

Travis called out to him, "Hey, Billy."

Billy turned and looked his way. A sheepish grin covered his face as he walked back towards Travis. "Hey, Travis, what's up, man?"

"You know what's up," Travis said.

Billy raised his hands in a surrendering pose and said, "I plead the Fifth."

Travis gave Billy a slight punch on his shoulder. "I called you and left several messages. What's up with you?"

"Sorry, so sorry. I did get the messages and meant to call, but I've just been a little busy, that's all."

Travis smirked and eyed Billy.

"Okay, okay, I know, I should never be too busy for family. My bad," Billy said.

A few fat raindrops started to fall.

"Come on, let's get to the car before we get drenched."

Both men walked quickly as they headed to Billy's car. Travis had almost walked past it, not realizing his uncle had a new car. Once they were inside, the rain started coming down in hard sheets, causing Billy to have to wait before attempting to drive in it.

Travis looked around the interior and took in the new car smell. "When did you get this?"

"Last week. You like it?"

Travis nodded his head. "Yeah, man, this is nice." The car had leather seats that made Travis want to sit in it forever and just relax. And he figured it must have had each and every upgrade that had been available.

"Why did you get another car?" Travis thought the car his uncle had before was nice.

"I was getting tired of that other car, and my girl has a son who just turned sixteen so I gave it to him as a present," Billy said.

Travis did a double take. "What, you just gave ol' girl's son a practically new car?"

"Man, that car wasn't new, and she ain't just ol' girl, she is my fiancée," Billy said.

"Say what?" Travis couldn't believe his ears.

"Yep, this player's days of playing are over. I am tired of running the game, trying to keep up with this one and that. Enough is enough. I'll be thirty-five next year."

Travis didn't think the player lifestyle sounded all that bad. It sounded better than the boring existence he was currently experiencing. "Wow, I can't believe you of all people are settling down." Travis shook his head. "What on earth is this world coming to?"

"I've let a lot of good women slip through my fingers in the past by playing my games," Billy said.

"These women play a lot of games too," Travis said.

"Not Ashley. She is a good woman and I am not going to let her get away." Then Billy chuckled.

"What's so funny?" Travis asked.

"Ashley actually reminds me a lot of Beryl," Billy said.

"What do you mean . . ." Travis's voice trailed off when he heard his uncle's cell phone ring.

Travis looked at the display on the ringing phone and saw a picture of a woman who looked pretty plain—short hair, minimal makeup, with a toothy smile.

Billy grinned. "Hold that thought," he said before answering.

As Billy spoke, Travis tried to wrap his mind around the fact that his best buddy was actually going to settle down and get married. He wondered how Billy was going to just give up the carefree life he'd been living. From Travis's point of view, Billy had it made. He had always been able to have his cake and eat it too.

After Billy clicked his cell phone off he said, "That was Ashley. That girl is something else. She told me to make sure I was home on time tonight for dinner, she has a surprise for me." Billy took a deep breath. "I love that woman."

"I know I must be having an out-of-body experience or something," Travis said. "Where is my uncle? What have you done with him? I know you are not using the L word."

"Yep." Billy grinned again. "That woman keeps it interesting."

"I guess you've got a hot night tonight," Travis said.

"With her there is no telling."

"Yeah, I'll just bet," Travis said. He knew his uncle very well.

"Oh, no, sir. It isn't what you are thinking with that nasty mind of yours."

"I know you know what I am thinking, 'cause I know how you are."

"Okay, since it seems as though I've blown your mind a couple times already, let me do so just one more time," Billy said.

Travis waited to see what else his uncle could say to possibly faze him.

"My fiancée isn't a virgin, of course, she already has a son, but she is and has been celibate since before I met her."

"Say what?"

Billy stared at Travis, letting him know he'd heard him correctly.

"Are you trying to say that you and Ashley have never been together?" Travis asked, his eyebrows rising in disbelief.

"Yep."

"I know you must have been abducted by aliens or something now."

"Nah."

"Well, it sounds like tonight might be your lucky night."

"Nah, doubt that. She has made it very clear that I won't be getting any until we are happily Mr. and Mrs."

"Well, dang. Wonders never cease. I just don't know what to say," Travis said.

As the rain let up some, Billy cranked the car and pulled off. "Speaking of which, what's up, man? I've got to get home."

Travis had almost forgotten about why he'd come to see his uncle in the first place. "I need a little favor." Travis figured if his uncle could afford a new car and to give one away, he must be doing pretty good and a couple hundred dollars shouldn't be a problem.

Billy pulled out of the parking lot and into traffic. "Yeah, what do you need?"

"I need to borrow a couple hundred dollars until next month."

"A couple hundred, huh?"

"Yeah, just until next month. It's been sort of hard having to try to make ends meet having to pay for this apartment all by myself," Travis said. He knew his uncle got the point. If Billy had not reneged on him to share an apartment, he wouldn't be scraping by like he was.

Billy rolled his eyes. "Okay, I'll have to see. Let me check with Ashley and I'll get back with you."

Travis did another double take. "Say what?"

"Yeah, Ashley and I have pooled our money together. We share the bills and expenses and if it were only a few dollars or maybe even twenty dollars or so, it wouldn't matter to me. But you're asking for a couple hundred."

Travis couldn't believe the words that were coming from his uncle's mouth. "Man, you act as if you two are already married or something. How are you going to just let her decide whether it is okay for me to borrow a couple hundred dollars?"

"Look, I know what you are thinking and she doesn't dictate anything. We've decided to make decisions together. So I don't mind letting you borrow the money, but I just need to let Ashley know about it. We are building our relationship on trust, and I am not about to break that trust before we can even say 'I do.'"

Travis held his hands up as if in surrender. "Okay, okay, I hear you." He didn't like what he was hearing, but he was glad his uncle was doing well and for once in his life the man was actually trying to do right by a woman.

"I'll talk to Ashley and get back with you." Billy looked down at the clock on his console. "Speaking of, I need to be heading home. I don't want to be late for dinner. Do you need me to drop you off somewhere?"

Travis needed to be taken back to his apartment, but it was on the other side of the city, so he asked Billy to drop him off at the strip mall that was just a couple of miles from his house. Maybe if he walked around the strip mall for a little the rain would die down so he could walk home.

"Take me to that strip mall over on Main Street."

As Billy drove over to Main Street, the men rode in silence. Travis tried to brainstorm on how he was going to get through the next month if Billy didn't lend him the money. Things just had to get better sometime soon. It seemed like every time he took a step forward he was somehow shoved two steps back.

When Billy pulled up to one of the stores of the strip mall, he stopped to let Travis out.

"Thanks, man. I hope you have a good night with your lady."

"I know I will. And I'll let you know what we decide about the loan," Billy said.

"All right. See ya," Travis said.

"See ya, nephew," Billy said. Then he pulled off like a man on a targeted mission.

Travis thought about going into the mall and picking up some applications to fill out for a job, but he didn't feel like it right then. He stepped into one of stores and acted as if he were actually looking for something to buy as he pondered his situation. Something had to give for him and soon. He was tired of struggling, tired of always doing the right thing but never getting any breaks.

After he had walked around the store a couple of times without picking up anything, one of the clerks in the store started eyeing him as if he were going to try to steal something. He rolled his eyes at her.

As he walked by one of the mirrors, Travis did a double take. His stomach was protruding way more than he remembered. He tried to suck it in, feeling like he had let his body go, all except for his teeth; he was pleased with the dental work he'd had done. He smiled at the mirror, showing his teeth. They looked good. Gone were his crooked teeth and the many gaps between them that haunted his childhood. The job he'd held working as a telecommunicator had provided him with great dental benefits. But soon after the work had been completed, he had lost his job due to staff cuts and now he still had pending dental bills looming over his head. But he thought it was worth it. He patted his belly and knew he was going to have to start exercising to get it back into shape.

He was glad his teeth were fixed, and with enough exercise he'd be able to get rid of his potbelly, but there was nothing he could do about his height. At only five feet, six inches tall, he considered himself short. In middle school and high school many of the guys picked on him, calling him short. Normally they did it in fun, as Travis would pick some aspect of their bodies to pick on. Like this one guy named Harold. Harold had big ears and Travis often called him Dumbo, like the cartoon elephant with the big ears. Then there was another guy named Jeremy who the guys nicknamed Stinky, because of the way his feet smelled, especially after PE classes.

And even though most of the name calling was in jest, he still had a complex, especially when it came to having to literally look up to women. Therefore, he rarely dated anyone who was taller than he was. But other than the height, Travis considered himself to be a very handsome, cocoa-skinned brother with smooth skin. He flexed his biceps and knew he really needed to start lifting some weights, also.

A few minutes later he heard a page being made over the intercom for security to scan zone five. He figured zone five was exactly where he was standing. Travis was sick of the racial profiling that he as a black man had to endure. And instead of arguing with the nosey clerk, he gladly left the store.

The sun looked as if it was about to finally peek through the clouds and Travis figured he'd go ahead and start his two-mile walk home. As he stepped off the curb to head to the street, a car came just inches from hitting him.

Travis was startled and so was the driver, who was opening his door to get out.

"Oh, my goodness, sir. Are you okay?" the man asked.

Even though Travis's heart was beating a mile a minute, he was physically okay. The car had not actually touched him. He wondered how he could have been so preoccupied not to have noticed the candy apple–red BMW 135i driving toward him.

After taking a couple of breaths, Travis looked at the man and told him he was okay and hadn't been hit. It was then that he realized the guy looked familiar.

"Brent?"

The guy must have noticed him at the same time because he immediately said, "Travis?"

"Ah, man, what's up?" Travis stepped toward the guy and the two hugged like long-lost Siamese twins.

"I can't believe this. I've been trying to find you for years," Brent said. "I looked on the social networking sites and everything."

"I'm not on any of those sites. Thought about setting up a page but never got around to it," Travis said.

The two men stepped up on the curb.

"I've been hoping I was going to eventually run into you or some of our other buddies from college," Brent said. "I didn't know that one day I might literally run into you," he joked.

"Glad to see you, but I have to say, I am glad you didn't run into me literally," Travis said.

"So how have you been? What have you been up to? Where are you living now?" Brent rattled off questions.

"Well uh . . ."

Brent cut him off. "Tell you what, let's grab a bite to eat; my treat since I almost mowed you down. Then we can catch up. Are you busy right now?"

Travis raised his eyebrows. "Ah, no. As a matter of fact I am free right now."

"Then come on, jump in, and we'll go grab something to eat. I can't wait to hear what you've been doing all these years," Brent said.

"Oh really? Well I can't wait to tell you," Travis said.

Chapter 2

Travis and Brent followed the hostess as she led them to their table.

"Your waitress will be with you gentlemen in just a few moments," the hostess said.

"Thank you," Brent replied.

"Thank you," Travis also said. He looked around at the swank five-star restaurant called Ginny's Brent had brought him to. Travis didn't think he had ever been to a restaurant as upscale as this one. Most of the people coming in, and who were already seated, looked as if they had money to burn. He doubted he'd ever see any of them at a McDonald's drive-through.

As soon as both men were comfortable in their seats, Brent commenced talking again. "It has been a long time. I hate that we lost touch after you left school."

"Yeah, you know my mom was having a hard time with paying my tuition, so I figured I'd just return home and take some classes at the community college. I did end up getting my associate's degree in general studies."

"Well good for you. I just completed my PhD in geology this past spring."

Travis loved his friend like a brother, but thought at times he was a little strange. He wondered what in the world the guy was going to do with a PhD in geology. He wondered how in the world the guy was supposed to make any money digging for some rocks all day.

"Congratulations on getting your PhD. So what are you doing now?"

"I am taking a little break. I'm about to go overseas and do some humanity work abroad. You know, to try to help others. We are so blessed here in the United States and there are so many others who are not as fortunate as we are."

As Brent spoke, Travis couldn't help but think that Brent was way more fortunate than even the majority of the people in the United States, period. Brent's parents were well-to-do, but most people wouldn't know it. They were millionaires but didn't carry the status with a wealthy air on their shoulders. Brent's mom was so down-to-earth that when his parents came up for a visit and took them out for lunch or dinner, the woman used coupons if she had them.

Brent never spoke much about the fact that his family was rich and Travis liked that about him. He also liked the fact that even though his parents were frugal in their spending, Brent, or his friends, never lacked for things during their days staying in the dormitory.

During the two semesters that Travis and Brent had roomed together freshman year, Travis never had to worry about how he was going to get around, never worried about getting hungry, and didn't even have to worry about books, because once Brent saw that Travis was having a hard time financially, he paid for Travis's books.

The guy was nice and down-to-earth just like his parents. Not once had Brent acted as if Travis was beneath him. And not once did he act as if Travis owed him for anything. And it seemed as though his friend was still the same as he had been all those years earlier as Brent was treating him to dinner.

Brent continued talking about all the things he'd been up to in the years since the two parted in undergraduate school. Travis sat listening and was especially enthralled as Brent talked about all the trips he had taken to various countries and the sights he had seen. Brent had even been to Hollywood, California.

Travis imagined going to Hollywood and finally being able to meet some of his most favorite movie stars like Blair Underwood, Denzel Washington, and Tommy Lee Jones. He'd love the chance to walk on a red carpet or ride down Rodeo Drive. Brent lived the life Travis was sure he was really meant to have.

All the while Brent spoke about his life and his adventures, not once did Travis feel like the man was bragging. The only feeling he got was that Brent, a true friend, just wanted to catch up with an old buddy. Brent spoke until the waitress came back with their appetizer, which was no surprise to Travis because even on campus years ago, Brent was known to be in many of the organizations and had even run for the student council freshman class president. What did surprise Travis was that Brent had not gone on later to run for political office.

It wasn't until Brent took a bite of his appetizer that he paused long enough to stop talking. Then he asked, "So what's going on with you? I tell you, man, I still can't believe I ran into you the way that I did." Brent took a sip of water. "I did see Craig once, but he didn't know how to contact you either."

"Craig Dawson?" Travis asked.

"Yeah."

Travis rolled his eyes. "Man, you know Craig would have been the last person I would have given a forwarding address to."

Both men laughed.

Brent nodded his head in agreement. "True that, true that. He was sort of an odd one, wasn't he?"

"That guy gave me the straight-up creeps. I used to avoid taking a shower when I knew we were the only ones in the bathroom."

Brent continued, "So tell me what big things you've got going on."

After all his friend had said about his exciting life, Travis knew his boring life couldn't compare. How could he tell this guy, who was so world traveled, that the closest he ever got to Europe was the European section of Busch Gardens in Williamsburg, Virginia, and that trip was over five years ago.

Even though he knew his friend wouldn't judge him, he couldn't tell him the truth about his job situation, the fact that he still hadn't actually received his paper degree for his associate's because he hadn't paid the final fees for the school, and that he was about to be evicted in a week if he didn't come up with the funds.

"Oh, me, well I've been dabbling in a little of this and a little of that. I was married but it just didn't work out. You know how that is." Travis didn't want to go into specifics about his marriage to Beryl, nor did he want to talk about his two little boys, Cameron and Jayden. He quickly added, "I just moved to Silvermont trying to see how I like the place. You know, just trying the city out—new scenery."

"I've traveled near and far, and I have to say, Silvermont has just as much or more to offer people as most of the other places I've been to," Brent said.

Travis figured Brent must have realized he hadn't really wanted to talk about his marriage because he hadn't acknowledged his saying anything about being married.

"Yeah, I don't know though, my lease at my apartment is about up and I might be looking to make another change. I just don't know if this city is right for me."

The waitress came with their entrees and both men dug into the food.

"So, you say your lease is about up?"

"Yeah, that's why I don't know if I am going to stay in the area."

Brent forked a piece of shrimp into his mouth. "Wow, isn't that ironic."

Travis took a bite of his lobster. "What is ironic?"

"You know I said I was taking a break to do some humanitarian work abroad."

"Yeah."

"Well, I have a house here in Silvermont. Mom and Dad bought it for me. I am playing with the idea of selling it but know my parents will not be pleased if I do." Brent took another bite of his shrimp. "Anyway, I'll be gone overseas for at least six months and I was trying to figure out what to do with my place while I was gone."

Travis listened, wondering what his friend was trying to say.

"I could pay someone to come in and water the plants and check on the house every now and then, but I would really feel more secure if someone really watched the place for me, so anybody looking for a house to loot won't be so tempted."

Travis nodded his head as he listened to his friend.

"I mean you know me. I am not really a materialistic person, but I do have quite a bit in my home and most of what I buy isn't cheap. So while I am not materialistic, I don't believe in wasting money, either."

Again Travis nodded his head.

Brent took another bite of shrimp. "So anyway, it is so ironic that you are here, a friend I trust, and you have a lease that is ending. Have you found another place yet?"

"Nah, not yet."

"Okay . . ." Brent's voice trailed off as if he was thinking about something. "All right, I have a proposition for you." He held his hand up to his friend. "Now just hear me out before you say anything."

Travis wasn't about to say a thing. Somehow he had a feeling that whatever Brent was about to say would somehow benefit him in a very good way.

"I am leaving in a week to go on this trip abroad. Like I said, I'll be gone for at least six months. And I was thinking since you already have a lease that is about to end, and you still want to check out Silvermont to see if it is a good fit for you, then why don't you house-sit for me? That way you don't have to get into another lease right away and it will give you time to decide whether you want to stay here."

Dropping his head, his mouth opened agape in a "say what" motion. Travis said, "Say what?"

"Wait, wait, just hear me out," Brent said, holding his hands up again. "I would feel comfortable with knowing I had someone I could trust looking after my place. And don't worry about having to pay rent or my mortgage or anything. I'll take care of that. Nor do you have to worry about the light bill or cable bill. I'll take care of those utilities too."

Travis couldn't believe his ears. He was speechless.

"The only thing I will ask is that you watch and take care of my place and mow the grass at least every other week and trim the bushes as needed. My homeowner's association can be pretty anal about the aesthetic appeal of the neighborhood. I have a mower and hedge clippers in my storage shed."

Sitting in utter disbelief, Travis took his hand and pinched himself on the leg under the table, trying to make sure he wasn't dreaming. The pinch hurt and he was very much in the here and now.

"So, what do you think?" Brent asked.

Travis shook his head slowly. "Man, I don't know what to say about an offer like that."

"Okay, you don't have tell me right now. Think about it. I know this is a pretty sudden thing to spring on you like that, but I was just thinking how perfect it would be for me." Brent wiped his hands on his cloth napkin. "Let it marinate overnight and let me know tomorrow if you can. I don't mean to put pressure on you, but I fly out in a few days and I'd sort of like to have things squared away."

"Okay, let me do that. Give me a night to think about it and I'll call you tomorrow and let you know." Travis didn't want to seem too eager, but then as he thought about it, he didn't want Brent to think he was totally uninterested in the idea. "To tell you the truth, it doesn't sound like a bad idea at all. I just need to do a few calculations, on my end, to see if it is something we can work out. I'll be sure to give you a call early in the day tomorrow."

Brent clasped his hands together in a clap. "Great." He stood. "I am going to head to the bathroom before we leave. I'll be right back."

Travis continued to sit in pure awe. He couldn't believe the proposition he'd just been offered. When the waitress came and set the bill down next to him, he quickly slid it over to Brent's side of the table.

Curiosity got the best of him and he slid it back to peek at the amount of their meals. Travis's eyes bugged when he saw the amount. The bill had come to a little over one hundred sixty-five dollars. He snapped the little folder shut and put it back down on the other side of the table.

A minute or so later Brent returned, picked up the bill, and glanced at it. Without flinching he pulled out his American Express card, slipped it in the folder, and set it back down for the waitress to retrieve. Then Brent pulled his cell phone out and asked, "What's your phone number?"

Travis told him the number. Brent dialed it and Travis felt the vibration of the phone in his pocket. He took it out, and looked at the caller ID to check and make sure the phone number had come through along with the call.

"All right, I've got your number," Travis said.

"Make sure now. Save it, don't lose it. I want to see your number come up on my caller ID tomorrow saying you have accepted my proposition." Brent chuckled.

Travis chuckled too. "Don't worry. I have a strong feeling you will not get disappointed."

After the waitress took the payment and returned with the receipt, Brent left the woman two ten dollar bills as a tip. Both men got up to exit the building and once they were outside the restaurant, Travis told Brent he'd forgotten his keys. He ran back inside to retrieve them, then met Brent back outside.

"So I can take you back over to the strip mall to your car if you'd like."

"Oh, my car is in the shop. Can you drop me off at home if you don't mind?"

"Sure. Where do you live?"

Travis gave Brent the address of his Uncle Billy's old apartment. He didn't want his friend to see the run-down apartments he was living in. And after Brent dropped Travis off and drove away, Travis headed to the bus stop.

He stood and waited with ten of the twenty dollars Brent had left for a tip at the table. Even though he felt bad about taking half the woman's tip, he didn't think she'd done that good of a job waiting on their table. Plus, it had gotten late and he needed the bus fare. So in his mind it was more than justified.

Travis had to get home to start packing his things. First thing in the morning he was going to call his friend and take him up on his proposal. Finally it seemed as though his luck was changing for the better.

Chapter 3

A week later, Travis still couldn't believe his luck. In just a few short hours he'd have a new address he would be calling home. Brent had picked him up from the car place at which Travis told him his car was being repaired. And he was now taking him over to his house for a tour. Brent needed to be dropped off at the airport and Travis told him he would take him but his car was in the shop. So Brent asked Travis if he wouldn't mind taking him in his car instead so he wouldn't have to pay the fees to park long term.

Travis gladly told him he didn't mind taking him and now Brent was pulling up into the garage of his home. The home was situated on a tree-lined street in a subdivision in which there were other similar two-story homes. When Brent had pulled up to the home, at first Travis wondered if he had pulled into the wrong place. With Brent being a bachelor, Travis figured the guy would be living in a little townhouse or at least a smaller home with a one-car garage, if that.

What Brent had pulled up to was a traditional-styled detached family home with a full front yard and a fenced-in backyard. The home had a full front porch big enough for rocking chairs and a porch swing. Brent opened up the garage and they pulled in. There wasn't another car in the other stall, and Brent had informed him that it would be fine for him to park his car in that spot.

They had entered the home through the attached garage.

"This is a nice home you have here, Brent," Travis complimented him.

"Thanks. Mom and Dad picked it out. I personally don't need all the space, but I think they are trying to think ahead, trying to tell me in a not-so-subtle way that they would like for me to settle down. My mom is always talking about how she would like to have some grandchildren before she is too old to enjoy them."

"Why don't you go ahead and make your mom's wish come true?" Travis asked.

"I will, all in due time. I wish Mom and Dad had gone ahead and had more children. This only child pressure gets to be a bit much at times," Brent said.

Travis couldn't understand why Brent was complaining; he wished his mom could have afforded to buy him a house. Shoot, right now he'd have been happy if his mother or the father he never knew would have been able to provide him with reliable transportation.

Brent looked at his watch. "Okay, I am making good time. Let me show you around and I'll give you the code for the house alarm, also. Pull your bags out of the trunk and I'll put my stuff in there; then we can head for the airport."

Travis was given a quick tour. Brent showed him the downstairs, which consisted of a foyer, living room, dining room, kitchen with an eat-in breakfast area, and a half bathroom. The foyer was the size of the living room area in his old apartment. Travis didn't see a television in the living room and was a little disappointed. He had seen the fireplace, but knew that he wouldn't need it during the few warmer months that he would be staying at Brent's place.

The upstairs consisted of three bedrooms and two bathrooms. Brent showed Travis the guest room that would be his for the next few months. To complete the tour, he showed him the other bedroom, which was used as an office, and Brent's master bedroom suite, which had a sitting area, a walk-in closet, and a bathroom with its tub separate from the shower stall. And the toilet had a privacy wall.

As Brent was telling Travis about the washer and dryer being on the second floor, he opened the door to another room. At first Travis thought he was opening the door to the washer and dryer, but realized there was another room situated over what Travis figured must have been the garage.

Travis's eyes bugged out when he stepped into this room.

"And this, my bonus room, is my man cave."

Travis stepped into the room. "I should say. Wow." He nodded his head as he stood in the middle of the room and turned around a full 360 degrees.

"Mom and Dad had originally put the TV, a couch, and a love seat in here. But I donated the couch and got chairs to replace it and the rest of the items you see in here."

There was a flat-screen television with a stereo system, and what looked to Travis to be all the games a man could wish for. There was a Sony PlayStation, the Nintendo Wii, and an Xbox. Sitting in the center of the room facing the large-screen television were two leather recliners, each with their own side tables.

"How big is that television?" Travis asked, his curiosity getting the best of him.

Brent's smile beamed. "Looks pretty nice, huh?"

Travis nodded.

"That, my friend, is a sixty-four-inch 3D plasma HDTV. And you should hear the surround sound on it. It makes it sound and feel like you are sitting right there in the movie theater."

"Man, I can't imagine," Travis said.

On the other side of the room Brent had a mini exercise room, with weights, a treadmill, and an exercise bike. He also had a mat, medicine balls, a jump rope, and a scale. And on one of the side walls, Travis saw something that made his heart race. Brent had a wall full of DVDs.

"This is really nice. You must be doing pretty good for yourself," Travis said.

"Oh, well I do all right. I just got that television last month as a graduation present for myself."

Brent showed Travis how to work the television and DVD player, and how to adjust to play mode for the games he had. Then he took Travis back downstairs where he showed him the backyard.

"Are you serious?" Travis asked as he looked around at all the bells and whistles the backyard held.

There was a deck that had two levels with a screened-in porch. Brent had a hammock, a man-made miniature pond, and an area in which Brent could practice putting his golf ball.

"See? I told you my parents are hinting hard." Brent smiled.

"I have to agree with you there."

"You see the back area over there?" Brent said as he pointed to the back corner of the yard.

Travis noticed that there was nothing there, in this almost-filled-to-capacity backyard. "Yeah."

"I believe my parents left that space for a play yard or something for kids. I am actually surprised they didn't buy one just to have it waiting."

Brent chuckled and Travis chuckled with him. But inside he thought what a lucky man his friend was. This was entirely too much space for one person. The space would have been more perfect for him, Beryl, and little Cameron and Jayden. He could just see his two little guys running around the backyard, trying to play tag and hide and seek.

Travis shook his head; he couldn't dwell on what would never be.

"Let me show you this before we head on back in to get the bags," Brent said.

He showed Travis the outdoor shed that held the yard equipment. "The mower should be full of gas, and the gas container, when you need it, is right here." Brent pointed to the gas can on the shelf. "So, if you can, cut the grass at least every other week. Like I said before, my homeowner's association can be a little anal when it comes to weeds and the height of the grass."

"No problem," Travis said.

Brent looked back at his watch again. "Okay, let's head on back in and get these bags situated."

The men walked back into the house and got Travis's bags first. Travis put his things in the guest room and then helped Brent put his things in the trunk of the car. Next, Brent showed Travis how to work the home security system and gave him a code to use. Lastly he handed Travis a set of keys to the house and the car.

"All right, let's roll." Brent headed for the passenger side of the car and got in.

Travis took this as his cue to get into the driver's seat. He slid in and closed the door and couldn't believe how good it felt to be in the driver's seat.

He cranked the car and looked around the steering wheel to make sure he knew where most of the buttons he needed were. Brent pointed out how to use the radio as well as how he could open the sunroof if needed. Then Travis pulled out of the garage.

Brent pushed the garage button and closed it back up. "You can just put this remote for the garage in your car to open and close it."

"Oh, okay," Travis said, knowing the only place he could put it right now would be in his pocket.

Travis continued to pull out of the driveway and headed for the airport.

Two hours later, Travis returned to the house. He'd stopped at the grocery store and picked up some food and a couple of personal items since he didn't know when he'd be venturing out again. He figured he'd make the stops while he was on the way home; better to justify driving the car by the store. He'd been careful the whole time, not wanting to get into an accident, much less put one scratch on another man's car.

As soon as he got inside he unloaded his groceries. He'd just gotten an unemployment check and the five bags of groceries he had were more than he had ever bought at one time since separating from his ex-wife. But now, since he didn't have to worry about paying rent that next day on April 1 or for the next eight months, he could afford it. He was glad, too, that he didn't have to think about owing any debts to the apartment complex since he had been on a month-to-month paying status and he had paid all of the late fees.

He opened the refrigerator and could have kicked himself. Brent had a refrigerator and freezer full of food. And Travis should have known the man would. Travis opened the cabinets and found food in them as well as matching sets of glassware and silverware, as well as cookware. Many of the items still looked brand new. Brent's mother was still probably treating him the same way she'd treated him when they were in college. He was sure she was probably the reason for Brent's kitchen being stocked the way it was.

Travis nodded his head, thinking that if Brent did ever find a woman, he wondered if she would put up with the degree to which Brent's parents, especially his mom, were so hands-on. Shrugging his shoulders, Travis commenced unpacking his groceries. As frugal as he had become, he wouldn't have to worry about shopping for groceries for a while. He had bought some theater-style microwave popcorn so he could sit in the bonus room and watch some movies. After popping the popcorn he opened up the bottle of Welch's Sparkling Grape Cocktail he'd purchased. He put a couple of ice cubes in a glass, poured himself a drink, and air toasted to himself, knowing this was an occasion to celebrate that called for way more than just grape Kool-Aid.

Chapter 4

Travis was on top of the world. For the first time in days he sat in peaceful silence. He knew there was no way life could get any better than what it was right now. He was sitting in the lap of luxury. He ran his hand across the leather recliner he was sitting on, and looked out of the window of the bonus room, in his home. Well, he knew it wasn't really his, but for the next six months he could and would refer to it as his home. Besides, his friend had said, *"Mi casa es su casa."* God had really been looking out for him right in the nick of time. Travis looked up toward heaven and mouthed a "thank you" to God. But somehow this small gesture did not seem like enough. He was going to have to make an effort to make it to church at some point in thanks for God's blessing.

But after a week and a half of wasting his time enjoying the luxury and finer things of life, he was starting to get a little restless. It was almost tax day, but Travis put that thought out of his mind. He hadn't filed taxes in years and wasn't planning on filing by the deadline in a couple of days either.

He'd watched movie after movie and when he needed a break from the movies he played games. Travis had eaten so much popcorn that the bonus room smelled like a movie theater. He was sick of it and didn't care if he saw any more anytime soon.

Once he tired of playing games he would turn the television on, enjoying the hundreds of satellite channels his friend had. He'd been able to catch up on more recent episodes of *The Biggest Loser*, and marveled over how real the people on television looked, not grainy as they had on his old-fashioned television. He'd left it on the curb, along with many of the other furniture odds and ends he'd purchased from the Salvation Army to furnish his apartment. He'd figured the items were probably still going to end up out on the curb, but because of God's grace he hadn't ended up on the curb with them. He wouldn't worry about that old stuff now, because if he budgeted and saved his money, he would be able to get some nicer things once he moved out of Brent's place. And maybe he would be able to afford a smaller version of the television Brent had. *I should be,* he thought. It was about time. After losing his wife, and another job, his luck was finally changing.

After picking up the remote and sliding his fingers over the buttons, Travis decided to forgo turning it on. He shook his head. Even though he wanted to look at the marathon that was running on cable with old episodes of *Law & Order,* Travis had more pressing things that were starting to nag his mind. He had six months to get his act together and if he didn't then, he might find himself out on the streets.

He was going to have to think of something to get out of the predicament he was in. If only his wife, Beryl, had stuck with him and given him another chance. He knew he would have been able to eventually find the right job. Then he would have been able to help pay the bills and get their second car fixed. But his wife hadn't kept the vows she'd said during their marriage ceremony. She said she would be there, "for richer or for poorer." She'd left him when hard times hit.

Although he didn't want to admit it, he missed having someone to talk to, and to love and hold. He missed those great home-cooked meals Beryl made, like the chicken and pastry. His mouth watered just thinking about her banana pudding. But most of all, he missed having someone to be his helpmate with the bills, when he was between jobs.

Other than food, shelter, and transportation, Travis thought about his other needs. The only thing he was missing was a woman. He wanted and needed a woman who was loving, and selfless, but also supportive. Someone who was down-to-earth and could hold her own if need be. But he didn't want someone so strong that she didn't want to be held in his arms when the time was right. He truly wondered if he would be able to find one woman with all those traits.

Travis thought about his Uncle Billy. Even though he had not met his fiancée, it sounded as if he and the woman had found a good thing in each other. They were working together toward common goals, so much so that his uncle hadn't called him back to say if he would or wouldn't be able to give him a loan.

Maybe that was what he needed. Maybe he needed to see if he could find someone with the traits that he wanted. It had worked for his Uncle Billy so why wouldn't it work for him? He tapped his fingers on the remote and thought long and hard about his situation. Six months seemed like a long time, but in truth, it could tick away faster than he could ever imagine. He was going to have to be smart. He was going to have to be resourceful. He was going to have to be whatever he had to be in order to get what he needed. If he didn't look out for himself, then nobody else would.

His cell phone rang. Looking at the caller ID, he saw that it was Beryl calling again. He hit the button to turn the ringer off. He wasn't in the mood to hear whatever she wanted to complain about today.

Instead he returned to his thoughts. Travis felt a plan forming in his head. He'd tried to play the good-guy role, but that had gotten him nowhere. The player lifestyle appealed to him, but so did the lifestyle his uncle was currently leading with his new fiancée. Travis made a decision. He was going to have to put himself into the game—the player's game. He was going to be a player, but one on a mission. Travis would do whatever he needed to do to find the right woman. He would look for someone who was the marrying kind.

The next day, Travis stepped off of the bus after riding it around for blocks as he tried to get a feel for the side of town he was now living in. He'd found the basic stores that he normally shopped at and had also found an area congested with fast-food restaurants. He'd made a note of where they were on the bus map he'd been using. He'd been pleased to be able to buy a thirty-one-day bus pass for only thirty-six dollars. With this he could ride an unlimited amount of times without worrying about being nickel-and-dimed.

The unlimited pass would give him the freedom to be able to get around and look for a job. The only thing he still had not been able to locate was a local library. He needed to be able to get on the Internet. With all the nice things Brent had in his home, he didn't have a desktop computer. And he had taken his laptop overseas with him.

He walked two blocks back down to a McDonald's he had seen. It was only a little before noon. He was hoping to find a daily newspaper someone might have left after reading it earlier that morning so he could look for job openings. He also made a mental note to ask someone about where the closest library was.

As he stepped into the restaurant he looked around at the tables and saw that, just as he had thought, someone had left a newspaper sitting on a table. He walked over, grabbed it, and placed it under his armpit. He then ordered a coffee with extra cream and sugar, then found a seat near the television.

He glanced over the headlines and a few of the local stories and saw an advertisement for a Sonnette concert coming to the city. Sonnette was one of his most favorite R&B singers. He wished he could go, but knew the tickets would be too high. And if he actually had a budget, he was sure it would be too high for it also. So he flipped on over to the want ads and started circling a few that looked like they had potential.

His cell phone rang. He looked at the caller ID and saw that it was Beryl, yet again. He wasn't going to answer. Most likely all she wanted was to know when he was going to send her some money for child support. He'd already told her time and time again that he was barely able to make it himself with the small amount he got paid in unemployment, but she never wanted to hear it. She was like a scratched CD repeating itself over and over again. Travis was tired of it.

He could normally gauge what kind of message Beryl might be leaving by looking at the message indicator. The indicator not only told him the name of the person leaving a message, it also told him how long the message was. This particular message from Beryl was a minute and twenty seconds. Travis knew she was probably telling him off for avoiding her and not contacting her. And he figured if there was an emergency with the boys, she would send him a text.

After circling five jobs that looked as if they might be promising, Travis folded the newspaper and stepped back up to the cash register to ask if anyone knew where the library was located. If he was able to get on the Internet, then he would be able to find out where the jobs were located in relation to the bus routes.

From the directions given by the cashier, the nearest local library was only about four blocks away. Travis got a refill on his coffee, added some more cream and sugar, and headed out to the library. As he stepped out of the McDonald's, he saw a petite, young African American lady with a dark-chocolate complexion standing outside her car with the hood up. She was dialing numbers on her cell phone, but didn't seem to be getting anyone to connect on the other end.

Travis walked over to her and asked, "Do you need any help?"

The young woman, who looked like she was in her late twenties, hunched her shoulders. "I don't know. The check engine light on my dashboard keeps flickering on and off. I don't know what is going on with this car. And I could be wrong, but my hood seems a lot hotter than it normally is."

Travis set his coffee on the ground and asked, "Do you mind if I take a look?"

As he said this he had a flash, back to the first time he and Beryl had met. Similar to this, she was having problems with her car. He'd helped her and later ended up getting married. Travis shivered at the thought.

"You okay?" the woman asked.

"Ah, yeah. Just remembered something, that's all," Travis said.

He looked around for the radiator coolant and saw that the level in the reserve looked fine. Upon touching the cap he felt that it was hot, so he didn't remove the cap. He also checked to see if she had any wires loose and then checked the level of oil. He pulled the stick out and saw nothing on it. He stuck it back in, then pulled it out and again did not see any oil registering on the stick.

"Young lady—"

The woman interrupted him. "You can call me Tory."

"Tory, huh?"

"Well, my name is Victoria, you know, like the girl on *Young and the Restless*. But my family and friends call me Tory."

"Family and friends, huh? Am I a friend now?"

Tory winked her eye.

"Well, okay then, Miss Tory."

She smiled to indicate he was right to call her "Miss."

"I don't really know if this has anything to do with why your check engine light keeps coming on, but you are about out of oil in your engine."

"Seriously?"

"Uh, yeah. Actually I didn't see any oil on the dipstick, so before I'd crank it and go anywhere else, I'd put some oil in it if I were you," Travis said.

"Ah, man."

Tory's cell phone rang. "Hello," she said.

As Tory spoke, Travis looked over the rest of her engine and even looked under her car and saw a couple of drops of oil.

When she finished her call, she said, "Great, my girlfriend is on her way over here. What kind of oil do I need? I know it will only be a Band-Aid on the situation but hopefully the oil will hold me over until I can get some money back from my taxes. I am going to file them tomorrow."

Travis thought about it. "Pick up a couple quarts of 10w-40. I am guessing you don't know what brand you normally use."

"Nope."

"For now you can probably get the store brand. It is normally cheaper than the brand names. And it looks as if you have an oil leak, so you probably want to get it to a shop as soon as possible."

He then pulled out the stick to show it to her. "Put about two quarts in then check the stick. See these two dots?" He pointed to two dots on the stick. "You want the oil to at least be between the two dots, not over the top one. If you still don't see any after you put the first two bottles in, you may need to put a little more in."

Tory placed her hand on Travis's shoulder. "Thanks. See, that's why I need a good man in my life to help me with all this mechanical stuff. I am clueless when it comes to cars."

Travis smiled, showing his pearly white teeth.

The woman's hand lingered for a moment before she finally took it away. "So you know my name; what's your name?"

"Oh, me? You can call me T.J.," Travis said, thinking he'd try out a new nickname.

"T.J.? What does that stand for?"

"The T is for Travis. And I think it just sounds better to add a J behind it. So you, my friend, can call me T.J."

"Well okay then, friend," Tory said.

A minute later, a car pulled up and the driver blew the horn.

Tory looked over at the car. "Oh, that's my girlfriend." She turned her attention back to Travis. "So, T. J., what do you like to do for fun?"

"I like to do lots of things for fun. What about you?"

"Oh, I do a little of this and that." Tory took her fore-finger and ran it down Travis's arm. "So, how can I contact you so we can find something fun to do together?"

Travis's eyebrows rose in question. He wondered if the woman was hitting on him. She winked her eye at him and he knew she was indeed hitting on him. He must still have had it, after all. He could still turn a woman's eye, protruding stomach and all.

He sucked his stomach in. "Maybe you could give me a call," he stated, testing to make sure he hadn't misunderstood the woman's intentions.

She pulled her phone out. "Sounds good. What's your number?"

Travis gave her his number. She punched it in and his phone vibrated in his pocket.

"Good, now you have my number," Tory said.

"Indeed I do."

"So you can call me sometime."

"Yes, I can."

"Thanks again for all your help. I look forward to talking with you again, soon." She winked at him again.

"That sounds like a good plan to me."

"Don't keep me waiting," Tory said.

Travis swallowed hard. He couldn't believe he was getting picked up by this young girl. "Can I ask you a question?" Travis said.

"Yes, what do you want to know, T.J.?" She said his name with a syrupy sweetness.

"How old are you?"

"Now you should know it isn't polite to ask a woman's age."

"I know, but I want to make sure you aren't jail bait." Travis chuckled a little. He felt relieved when Tory did the same.

"Oh, please, I am nobody's jail bait, but thanks for thinking so. I'll have you know I am twenty-nine years old."

"You're lying." Travis's eyebrows rose in disbelief. She didn't really look a day over twenty-eight to him.

"No, sir, I am not. How old are you?"

"Thirty-six."

She playfully hit his arm. "Shut up. No, you are not."

Travis smiled, thinking that the woman really knew how to boost a man's ego. "Yes, I am."

"Well, I like older men, so don't you worry about any age thing."

"If you aren't worried then I am certainly not worried," Travis said.

"Well, I gotta go. Call me." She used her remote to lock the doors on her car and walked around to the passenger side of her friend's car.

"You'll hear from me soon, I promise."

She smiled and got into the friend's car. As the friend drove off, Tory waved with her fingers.

After they were gone Travis reflected on the last fifteen minutes. His plan to become a player seemed to have started on its own without any extra forethought of his own. In his head he could hear J. Anthony Brown from the Tom Joyner radio morning show saying, "Playa, playa, play on!"

Chapter 5

"Yes, sir. I can be there at eight in the morning on Wednesday. Thank you," Travis said, pressed the button to end the call, and sat back down on the recliner in the bonus room.

After almost a week of diligently searching for a job, making a point to put in at least two applications per day, he finally received a phone call and the manager wanted him to start that Wednesday. He was going to be working at a local fast-food restaurant working as a cashier. With all the jobs he'd had in the past, he had never actually worked in the fast-food industry. But he had eaten his share of fast food, and figured there couldn't be much to it. Most of the stuff he'd seen from ordering food involved dropping fries in a basket and flipping burgers on a grill. *So how hard could all that be?* he thought.

He had one more day of freedom until he was back into the workforce. He'd make sure to enjoy it to its fullest. As he pondered how he could fill his day, his cell phone rang again. It was a number he didn't recognize. He answered it.

"Hello?" he greeted in question.

"Well, hello, stranger," the sweet voice said over the receiver.

Travis knew exactly who it was. "Hello, Victoria," Travis said.

"Now what did I tell you about calling me Victoria? My friends call me Tory. And I thought you were my friend."

"I am your friend. I guess in some ways I am a little old-fashioned. Sorry about that, Miss Tory," Travis said.

"Now that's more like it, T.J." She giggled. "I hope I didn't disturb you. I am on my lunch break and I just thought I'd give you a call to see how you were doing since you hadn't called me."

Travis loved the way Tory spoke his new nickname. And he loved the sweetness of her voice. "Tory, I'm sorry I haven't called. I was going to give you a call this evening for sure."

"Well, look, I won't hold you long. I didn't really want to disturb you at work," Tory said.

"No worries, this is my day off."

"Oh, okay, well good then. What are you up to tonight?" she asked.

"I hadn't made any plans. What about you?"

"Well, on first Mondays, Rollerland has an adult skate party. Admission is free before nine, and all you have to pay for is the skate rental. What do you say? Do you want to meet me out there?"

"Rollerland, huh?"

"Yep."

"Where is that exactly?"

"It's off Ridge Road."

Travis racked his brain trying to remember if he'd seen Ridge Road on his bus map. "Is it in the same shopping center as the Super Target and the Costco warehouse?"

"Yeah," Tory said.

Travis thought about it. He had his unlimited bus pass, and all he had to pay for was the skates. He wouldn't even mind splurging for Tory's skates since he was now able to retain more money due to his new housing situation. It sounded like a good idea. He needed to get out with other adults and have some fun.

"Sure, what time do you want to meet?" Travis asked.

"How about eight o'clock? That will give me time to get home and freshen up a little."

"Sounds good to me. I'll meet you there at eight o'clock," Travis said.

After they were off the phone Travis looked out of the window, thinking he heard a car pulling up in the driveway. He saw a truck turning around. He noticed that the grass looked like it was getting a little high, but thought it was too hot to get out in the yard right then. He decided to get up early in the morning to cut it instead.

Starting to feel a little sleepy, he decided to take a nap so he would be refreshed and ready for his night of rolling around. After grabbing a blanket from the linen closet, he got comfortable on one of the recliners and easily drifted into sleep.

When Travis awoke from his nap, he felt refreshed and ready to rock and roll with Tory. He showered, put on a pair of jeans and a T-shirt, and splashed on some cologne just before grabbing his wallet and bus pass.

He'd just made it to the bus stop before the bus pulled up. His timing couldn't have been better. The bus had ended up taking him straight to the shopping center. He was glad not to have had to do any bus transfers. That would make it easy when it came time to get back home later that night. According to the bus schedule, the last bus left at 12:30 A.M., so if he wasn't careful he'd be like "Cinderfellow", minus the pumpkin.

As he stepped off the bus, Travis saw quite a few people standing outside waiting to get on the bus. He figured this particular event must be pretty popular. He craned his neck around looking for Tory but didn't see her. His cell phone made the familiar jingling sound that indicated he had a text message.

Upon looking at his phone, he saw he'd missed a call from Tory and a voice mail. The text message said that she was inside the skating rink. She told him she was wearing a sunshine-yellow jumpsuit, and he wouldn't be able to miss it.

And sure enough, by the time he finally made his way through the line and the crowd of people gathered by the entrance of the rink's front door, he saw Tory sitting at a booth by the concession stand with two other women. There was no way anyone could have missed her. Her jumpsuit was indeed a bright sunshine yellow, from top to bottom. On anyone else, he thought it probably would have looked outlandish, but Tory wore it well. Travis did think that it was something that might be a little young for the woman to wear, but who was he to judge?

He stepped up behind her and tapped her on the shoulder.

She turned and offered a big smile, her disposition matching her sunny choice of clothing. "Hey, T.J." She jumped up and gave him a hug, then turned to the friends she was sitting with and said, "This is the guy who saved my life last week."

Travis smiled. "I wouldn't say all that."

Tory looked him up and down. "Glad you could make it. These are my friends Melissa and Jackie." Both the young women waved at Travis. They, like Tory, looked as if they were barely out of high school.

Tory stood. "Come on, let's go get you some skates so we can get on the floor." She tugged at Travis's arm. She rolled on her skates and he walked his way through the crowd.

After he had his skates securely tied, Tory then pulled him out onto the packed roller rink floor. He had to dodge a couple of people to keep from getting hit. Tory released his hand and zoomed ahead of him. With more effort than he had ever remembered in past years of skating, Travis did his best to lift his legs with the skates that felt like they'd been plated with lead. It felt as if he had only gone a couple of feet before Tory rolled back by his side.

"T.J., are you okay out here?" she asked.

"Yeah," Travis yelled over the thumping R&B music. "It's just been awhile since I've been on roller skates, that's all."

"I see," Tory yelled over the music and the sound of people skating past them.

When they rounded a curve, Travis made an effort to pick up speed, and found that he could go a lot faster than the creeping pace he'd started at. He was pretty pleased with himself, and Tory smiled as she slowed down to keep pace with him.

He thought about the days when he was a teenager and went to the skating rink with his friends on the weekends. Back then, he skated forward, backward, not only standing high but also squatting down. All of his maneuvers were effortless back then.

When Travis got to the next curve in the rink, he found he was moving too fast. He wasn't going to make the turn in the curve in time. He tried to stop himself with the foot stopper on his skates and ended up flying headlong into the wall. He'd narrowly missed hitting a couple who were holding hands as they skated around the rink.

For a couple of seconds, Travis could have sworn he saw stars. He saw concern in Tory's face when she reached him. She and the guy from the couple who were holding hands helped him stand.

"T.J. Are you all right?" Her face was still wrought with concern.

Travis took a deep breath. His head and shoulder hurt immensely. The DJ had stopped the music, and one of the workers came over to ask if he was okay. It felt as if every eye in the place was on him.

"Yeah, yeah. I'm fine." Travis brushed his clothes off as if removing imaginary dirt. He was embarrassed to say the least. Not only had Tory watched him crash into the wall, so had many others. And now it looked like he was some idiot who didn't know how to skate.

He whispered to Tory, "I'm going to head to the bathroom for a minute."

"Okay, do you want me to skate with you over there?"

"Nah, I got this."

Since no one was skating, waiting to see how hurt he was, Travis took the opportunity to skate in the opposite direction from where he had originally been going. The bathroom was in that direction. He hoped getting to the bathroom would make him out of sight, thus out of mind and focus for the crowd of onlookers.

With his head held high Travis skated on toward the restroom. His pace was faster than it had been when he first started out on the rink floor, but not nearly as fast as it had been just before he flew into the wall.

Once he passed through the doors of the bathroom, he was pleased to hear the music resume, and was also glad that the bathroom was empty. He looked at the top of his head in the mirror to see if a lump had formed.

And, sure enough, he saw a raised, reddish-looking area where he'd had the most impact with the wall.

He rubbed the spot and it was extremely tender to the touch. He knew he'd probably have a doozie of a headache in the morning when he got up. He also touched his right shoulder with his left hand. It too was tender to the touch.

Another guy entered the bathroom and made eye contact with Travis. Travis acknowledged the guy with a head nod and the guy did the same. That was the extent of it. The guy commenced to handle his business, and Travis went about his own business before leaving the restroom. He wasn't exactly sure how much time had passed. A couple of songs had played and he figured Tory was probably wondering where he was. He held his now throbbing head up high and set out to see where Tory was.

Again, he found her sitting in the snack bar area. As soon as Tory saw him she skated up to him. "Oh my goodness, T.J. Are you okay? Come on, have a seat."

"I'm okay, I'm okay," Travis said.

"Are you sure you're okay?" one of Tory's friends asked. "You hit that wall pretty daggone hard. I saw the whole thing." The woman cringed as she spoke.

"Yeah," said the other friend. "Your head has got to have a crack in it, to say the least."

Women were so nurturing. Travis thought about the contrast between them and how the guy in the restroom acted. The guy hadn't said a word to him to see how he was or wasn't doing, and all three of these women were trying to play doctor. He smiled back at them. "Ladies, I assure you I am fine."

The desire to roller skate or to socialize was no longer felt by him. All he wanted to do was to get back to the house and take some pain medication. His head throbbed more and his body was already starting to become sore.

He turned to Tory. "Hey, I think I'm going to just call it a night."

Looking at him with concern, Tory stood. "Are you going to be okay? Do you want me to see you home?"

"No, no," Travis said. He didn't have any desire to explain why he was riding the bus and didn't have a car. He glanced at his watch. There was more than enough time to catch a bus and get home.

"Are you sure?" Tory frowned.

"Yeah. I'll be fine. Don't worry or frown like that." He put his hand on her cheek. "That frowning does not become you."

Tory smiled. She went to reach for her purse. "It's no problem. I can hang out with these chicks anytime."

"No, no. I'll be fine. I'll send you a text when I get home to let you know I am okay," Travis said, then left the rink and headed home.

As soon as Travis got home he headed for the medicine cabinet. He pulled out a bottle of 600-mg ibuprofen and took one. He then took a long, hot shower. After drying off and putting the towel around his midsection and bottom, he headed toward his bedroom. He put on some underwear and a T-shirt.

Upon looking at the clothing that he had flung on his bed earlier, he dreaded having to move it. So he decided to sleep on the recliner in the bonus room. But when he passed Brent's bedroom and looked at the inviting king-sized bed, he figured it wouldn't hurt anything to sleep in there for the night; after all, this was his home for now.

Chapter 6

Travis's eyes fluttered open as a bright light shined in his face. When he looked over to see the source of the light, he saw that it was a beam of light from the sun coming in through the curtains. He shifted his head slightly. For a few moments he didn't know where he was. As he continued to try to turn his body away from the light, thoughts of the night before flooded his memory.

He let out a groan from the pain he felt in his shoulders and in his head. His legs and backside also felt sore. "This is not going to work," Travis gruffly whispered to himself.

Looking over at the clock on the nightstand, he saw that it was already after ten o'clock in the morning. His stomach grumbled. With reluctance he pulled the covers off and stiffly made his way down to the kitchen to grab something to eat. He scrambled eggs, made some grits, and warmed some pieces of cold cut ham. It was the closest breakfast he could make that even remotely resembled a down-home Southern breakfast.

After eating he took another 600-mg ibuprofen. Within the hour his headache subsided and his limbs didn't feel as sore. He cringed as he thought about his fumbling attempts to skate around the skating rink. And although he hadn't really fallen on his legs, they were still tense. Plain and simple, Travis knew he was out of shape. All those days of eating quick-processed, high-carbohydrate, high-sodium, and high-fat foods while sitting in front of the television had finally caught up with him. How did he actually expect to attract many women with the spare tire he'd acquired around his waist and the flab on his arms?

In his guestroom he riffled through the clothing on the bed and found a pair of shorts and a wife-beater T-shirt. He pulled on a pair of socks and his sneakers, then headed to the home gym in Brent's bonus room. He wasn't going to let his sore limbs get the best of him.

He started with the exercise bike to get his blood flowing, then moved on to the free weights and did repetitions that worked many of his muscle groups, especially his biceps, triceps, and his deltoid muscles. He also worked his abdominal muscles by doing diagonal chops, crunches, and standing oblique twists. When he was done with all the other exercises, he jumped rope and finished the workout by doing fifty pushups. Afterward he drank what seemed like a gallon of water, and took a shower to wash off all of the sweat that had been pouring from his pores.

Travis was truly pleased with his accomplishment. If he could get some minutes in each day doing various exercises, then he'd have his lean body back within a few months. When he moved his arms now there was still some tenderness, but he could take it. After working out a few more days, he knew, all the tenderness would go away anyway. He just needed to stay in the swing of things.

By the time he finished showering, it was almost three o'clock in the afternoon. Travis was exhausted. He headed to the kitchen and turned on the radio on the TV/DVD/radio combination Brent had affixed to the bottom of his cabinets. In the kitchen he fixed himself a turkey and cheese sandwich with mustard instead of mayonnaise, to cut down on the fat content of the food, and opted to drink some water instead of his grape Kool-Aid. He was going to be serious about getting back into shape.

He bopped his head back and forth with a tune that had just finished playing on the radio. Then he listened to the DJ on Foxy 107 as he told listeners to be listening out for the song "The Moment" by the music artist Sonnette. When the song played it would indicate they were looking for the seventh caller to win tickets to see Sonnette. Sonnette was one of the newest and hottest acts rising on the R&B charts. Travis liked all kinds of music, especially gospel and R&B. He wasn't really into rap that much since nowadays it seemed as if the rappers weren't like they were in the days of his youth. It seemed like the rap he'd heard lately on the radio was just jumbled words with a fair enough beat, but nothing too memorable.

Travis commenced sitting at the bar in the kitchen to eat his late lunch. His stomach and bladder both seemed to fill at the same time due to all the water he'd been drinking. He ascended the stairs to use the bathroom. When he returned to the kitchen to clean up his dishes, he heard Sonnette's song playing. He quickly patted his pants for his cell phone, but it wasn't there. He remembered it was upstairs in his bedroom.

He took the stairs two at a time to get to his phone. Then he punched the speed dial for the radio station. As he returned to the kitchen he heard the radio announcer stating that he had the seventh caller, and a guy with a deep baritone voice conversed with the DJ, trying to find out if he was the winning caller. The DJ bantered back and forth with the guy and finally told him that he was the seventh caller. The man yelled into the phone in disbelief, stating that he'd been wanting to take his wife to the concert but the tickets had been sold out for weeks. He thanked the DJ, who told him to hold on the line so that he could get the rest of the man's information.

Travis shook his head, hoping they would give away some more tickets for the show. The next time he went to the bathroom, he was going to have to turn the radio up so that he could hear what songs were playing. If he could score tickets to the concert then he could ask Tory if she wanted to go. He'd just have to work out the logistics on how to get to the concert.

His cell phone rang as soon as he set it down. After looking at the caller ID and feeling pretty assured that it wasn't Beryl calling, he answered the call. It was the manager of a local restaurant called Fries and More, which was a fast-food establishment. Travis told the manager he could be at work bright and early the next morning.

After hanging up, he felt like he was back on a roll again. All the work he had done putting in applications during his visit to the library was finally paying off for him. Once again he would be gainfully employed, which was a good thing because his unemployment checks were about to run out soon.

That next morning Travis awoke again in Brent's bed. Similar to the morning before, getting up had been a struggle, one because he was still tired, and also because his body was now doubly sore. He figured it was a combination of the fall he took at the skating rink and all the exercise he'd done the day before. He realized he must have overdone it.

Moving with the speed of an eighty-five-year-old man, Travis painfully took his shower, got dressed, and trudged his way to the bus stop. Every step and movement hurt his body. It hurt to walk, it hurt to move his arms, and at times it even hurt to breathe. And when he sat down on the seat of the bus, even his backside hurt and he dreaded having to get back up later and continue his painful walk to the restaurant.

For a fraction of a second he contemplated just saying the heck with it all and going back to the house. But he had no idea when someone else might offer him another job, so he continued on to the Fries and More restaurant.

Soon after Travis arrived at the restaurant, the manager gave him his uniform and trained him on the cash register. For the first hour or so, he watched his new boss, Benny, take orders like the seasoned Fries and More manager he was. It all looked simple enough to Travis. Next the manager left Travis so that he could take orders on his own. He had done his fair share of eating at many fast-food restaurants in his day so he really thought it would be easy, but he was wrong.

When Travis stepped up to the counter to take his first order by himself, he adjusted the tie around his neck. The uniform he was wearing was too tight. The tie felt like it was choking his neck. And it didn't help that his body was already sore, either.

He smiled at an Asian woman who had walked up to place an order. "Welcome to Fries and More, where we have fries, burgers, chicken, and more. What would you like to order today?" Travis asked, saying the slogan that the restaurant's employees were mandated to say.

"Ah, yes, I would like a chicken sandwich, with mayonnaise, cheese, and lettuce. I don't want any tomatoes or onions or pickles. Also give me a junior-sized fry and a medium cola. Also I want an apple pie, but I don't want it heated," the woman said.

Travis looked at the cash register and was still trying to type in what the woman wanted on her chicken
sandwich. He was pretty sure the sandwich didn't
come with cheese and he'd have to add it somehow,
and that the sandwich already didn't come with pickles
or onions, but was not sure about the tomatoes. He
fumbled with the screen. *Why couldn't the lady have
just ordered a combo number two?* Travis thought.

He put the order in and hoped he had gotten it right.
The woman looked impatient and he didn't want to get
his head bitten off by asking her to repeat the order.
So he stepped over to the fry station, slower than he
normally would have due to the pain he felt with each
move. He scooped up the junior fries for the woman.
Then he took steps over to the soda fountain and got
her drink ready to allow the cook to complete the spe-
cial-order chicken sandwich.

Once the sandwich was ready, he placed it in a bag
along with the fries and the drink. When the woman
took the bag from Travis she checked it and asked
where her apple pie was. Travis apologized and got the
pie for her. As soon as he handed it to her she frowned.

"I wanted my pie cold, not hot," the woman said. She
handed it back.

Again Travis apologized. He'd totally forgotten the
woman wanted the pie cold. He turned and asked the
cook for a cold pie, and handed it to her. She was being
a pain, literally and figuratively.

She placed it into her bag and frowned again. "My
fries are cold."

"Oh, sorry about that," Travis said. He returned to
the fry area. Someone had dropped a basket in the
grease and the light to indicate that they were ready
to be taken out was blinking. He pulled the fries up,

poured them in the fry bin, and scooped up another junior fry for her.

When he turned back to the counter, he saw a full scowl on the woman's face.

"I want to see a manager, now," the woman said with more force than Travis thought was warranted.

Benny appeared from nowhere it seemed and asked, "Is there a problem?"

"Ah, yeah." With an attitude, the woman pointed at Travis. "This guy has completely gotten my order wrong. First my apple pie was missing, and when he finally gave it to me it was hot. I wanted it cold. Then he gives me cold fries. And to top that all off, luckily I checked my sandwich and it's missing the cheese."

"Miss, I am sorry for your inconvenience. I'll take care of this for you." Benny took the bag from the woman, looked at the receipt, and asked her exactly what she wanted. He told the cook, and then got another cold pie for the woman, and hot fries and a fresh cola for her also.

Within two minutes Benny had the correct order for the woman. He slipped a coupon in her bag so that she could come back to receive a free fry with her next burger order. The woman was on her way out of the door, still frowning but sufficiently appeased. During the entire transaction, Benny hadn't said anything negative to Travis, nor had he reprimanded him, he just smiled and encouraged him to take the order of the next customer in line.

For the next hour, Travis took orders and only got about half of them completely right. After another person complained about her food, Benny decided to move Travis to the back to assist the cook with orders and to help the other cashiers with making sure the fries and onion rings were hot and plentiful.

"You see, Travis, Fries and More strives for good, quality food and customer service. Customer service does not end at the counter; it also goes into the food we put into our customers' bags. We want the orders to be right, fast, and hot, especially the fries," Benny said.

Travis nodded his head in understanding.

Travis heard them before he saw them. It was a bus full of children in for the lunch hour. He figured they must have stopped in the middle of the day in the midst of some sort of field trip. He was glad not to have been standing at the cash register. But that gladness was short-lived as the orders started coming for the forty-two kids' meals and the adult meals for the chaperones and teachers.

He had to help with dropping the fries and onion rings as well as with the fish fillets, chicken fillets, sliced roast beef, and mozzarella sticks. And for a little while, during the time the cook had to run to get supplies from the outside shed, Travis had been tasked to flip burgers. He almost started wishing he was back on the register.

With every burger he flipped and basket of fried food he had to drop, his arms and body continued to ache. And though he willed his body to move faster, his speed was way slower than it would have been on a normal day.

During the first few minutes of the orders coming in, Travis did pretty well. But when the orders started coming in even quicker he started messing up big time. He accidentally dropped the fish fillets in the oil designated for the fries. A couple of customers complained that their fries tasted like fish. He also had people complain about the amount of roast beef on their sandwiches, saying there was not enough on them, because he had not been paying attention to what size sandwiches people were ordering. Then he made the mistake of keeping the mozzarella sticks in the oil for too long, as well.

Benny, who had gone on a break just before the crowd of people came in, saw what a mess Travis was making as soon as he walked into the kitchen. Travis could tell the man was not pleased by the look of disbelief on his face. Travis figured one of the other employees had probably gotten to Benny and told him about the mayhem he was causing.

It wasn't until the entire shift was over that Benny let Travis know that he didn't think the fast-food business was for him and he strongly encouraged him to look for work in another type of industry. When Travis asked about the paycheck for that day of work, Benny told him that he could come by to pick it up in two weeks.

The whole fiasco made him feel as if he were on an episode of *Hell's Kitchen* due to the glares he was getting from his coworkers about all the mistakes he'd made. And when Benny let him go, it felt like he was being told to take his apron off—just like they did on the show.

It wasn't all bad, though. Benny had been one of the nicest people he had ever been fired by, and Travis had been fired by many bosses. Benny was professional in his manner and Travis appreciated that. Because of Benny's demeanor Travis would continue to be a patron of the business. And as he left through the doors of the restaurant, he had a newfound respect for people working in the fast-food industry.

As Travis got himself settled on the bus for the ride home, he checked his cell phone and saw that he had a voice mail message. When he checked it, there was a message from a guy named Andre asking him to call back for a job offer.

Travis returned the call. Andre told him that he had an opening for a car washer. Travis would be detailing cars at the Silvermont Wash and Dash. He was told that the Wash and Dash was known for washing and detailing cars at record speeds so that customers could quickly get their cars cleaned and be on their way.

Gladly, Travis told the guy that he could start that Friday. He didn't want his body to still be sore on his first day of work there. Luck was truly on his side. He'd just gotten fired and now he was gainfully employed once again.

Chapter 7

Andre showed Travis around the Wash and Dash. And then let him observe the Wash and Dash process to see how it worked. The manager showed him the time frame that was normal for the basic Wash and Dash package to be completed in.

Travis watched in amazement as a car pulled up, the driver got out, and it was driven over to a car wash area. Before the driver of the vehicle was in the door of the waiting room, a group of eight Wash and Dash employees, wearing their purple and green Wash and Dash uniforms, had descended on the car.

Each person was responsible for certain areas on the inside; then once done with the details of the inside they cleaned the outside. It reminded Travis of the pit crews he'd seen on television during races as they changed tires and quickly added gas to the cars.

"Many of our customers come through wanting the basic package," Andre said after he'd shown Travis the layout of the place.

Travis nodded his head.

"Others want custom services and want to feel like they are getting a more tailored treatment." Andre pointed at the sign with the packages and prices. "There is the silver package, the gold package, and the platinum package. And as you can see each package builds on the services that are offered and the prices for those services."

Again Travis nodded.

"The guys around here like to joke that the basic package should be called the scrap metal package." Andre laughed.

Travis laughed also. But he wasn't laughing because what Andre said was funny, but because Andre had a funny laugh. Andre looked a bit like a laughing hyena and now that he was actually laughing, the man sounded like one as well. A couple of the customers in the waiting area glanced over as Andre laughed, and Travis knew he wasn't the only one thinking what he was thinking.

Andre acted as if he didn't have a care in the world, and as if not too much really bothered him. Travis thought that it might be nice to work for someone who wasn't too uptight. He'd worked with enough people like that in his life.

Travis was given a Wash and Dash uniform to put on. The uniform of khaki shorts and the cotton short-sleeved shirt fit him so much better than the uniform from his previous job. He actually felt as if he could move around freely in the outfit. He also liked the fact that he didn't feel closed in at the car wash.

Andre watched Travis as he was given a couple of cars that had been left by a company to be detailed. Because the company wouldn't be there to pick them up until the next day, there was no need for Travis to rush. His boss mainly wanted to see how Travis worked and if he had an eye for detail.

The cars didn't seem too dirty to Travis, but he made sure to vacuum every nook and cranny and made sure to wipe down each and every crevice he could find. He'd cleaned the windows, making sure there wasn't a speck of dirt or a fingerprint smudge. When he was done he was pleased with his handy work.

Once he was finished, Andre gave him the thumbs up. Travis thought the guy was bordering on the corny side. He didn't really care, though, because watching how his new boss acted provided entertainment for him.

Later in the afternoon, Travis had just come back from lunch and Andre pulled him to the side and told him that they had a customer who needed the Barbie package. When Travis asked what the Barbie package was, because he hadn't seen it on the board, Andre rolled his eyes.

"The Barbie Package isn't really a package. We have a few customers who want touchups between car detailings and because they come so frequently we cater to them. I called it a Barbie package because it is a woman who wants her touchup. When it is a guy we call it the Ken package," Andre said; then he laughed.

Travis did his best not to laugh this time. He really didn't want to prolong Andre's laughing.

"So, I need for you to do a few touchups on that BMW over there. Wipe down the interior, redo her windshield and other windows, and spray a little of this fragrance in there." Andre handed Travis a little bottle of spray.

Andre looked over toward the waiting area where he nodded to a woman dressed in skin-tight jeans and a fuchsia baby T-shirt. Her hair, which Travis figured wasn't naturally hers, hung down to her mid-back area.

Travis didn't realize he was staring at the woman until Andre tapped him on his arm and said, "Come on this way. Here are the keys."

He followed Andre over to a sleek black BMW X5. As he walked up to the SUV Travis admired the shine coming off of the vehicle, the tinted windows, and the fog lights. And upon opening the car his mouth salivated over the soft leather seats, the sunroof, and the satellite radio. As he cleaned while looking for nonexistent smudges and dirt, Travis imagined himself driving in the car, with the sunroof open, while listening to some smooth jazz.

His hand accidentally hit the glove compartment and opened the dashboard as he cleaned around it. The inside held a mini flashlight, a pair of gloves, and the car registration. Instead of quickly closing the glove compartment, Travis looked around to see if anyone was watching him. When he saw that no one was paying him any attention, he examined the car registration more closely. The name on the registration was Jade Morris. She lived at 61 Lafayette Street in Silvermont.

He didn't remember seeing a Lafayette Street on any of the bus maps or the city map he had used before. He figured that with the way the woman was dressed and the car she drove, she might not live in an area that had public bus transportation.

He placed the registration back in the glove compartment and closed it back up. "Jade Morris, huh?" Travis whispered to himself, thinking it was a pretty name for a very attractive woman. Then he imagined driving down the highway with Jade in the passenger seat.

When he heard a tap on the window, Travis figured he must have been daydreaming for too long, because there was a frown on Andre's face. "Travis, are you done yet?"

Travis opened the door. "Yeah, I was just finishing up." He took a cloth and wiped the window where Andre had just knocked with his knuckles.

"Okay, little Miss Barbie is getting impatient over there," Andre said.

Travis smiled over toward the woman, who hardly paid him any attention as she looked down at her watch with impatience. He handed Andre the keys back.

The rest of the afternoon, Travis worked helping with gold, silver, and platinum package jobs. Andre had told him that as he got better with those jobs, he would be able to move up to be one of the purple crew: the guys who did the Wash and Dash basic package speed clean. Throughout the afternoon, Travis thought about Miss Jade Morris. He figured she was indeed a Miss because she wasn't sporting a wedding ring or even an engagement ring.

The Wash and Dash was open seven days a week. For six days straight Travis worked and learned how to properly detail cars to the specifications of the Wash and Dash corporate office. He was given a day off, on a Friday; then, the next day, when he came back, Andre moved him up to the purple crew. He was given the task of cleaning and washing the back right side passenger area of the car.

When the first car rolled in, he was ready and raring to go. He pulled the door open, pulled out the mats just as he had seen the other guys do, then he commenced vacuuming the back seat, the floor, and under the front passenger seat, then started vacuuming the mat that he'd previously pulled out.

As he glanced at the other guys who were bound and determined to be the first ones finished with their sections, Travis pushed himself to go even faster. He loved a challenge. He placed the mat he was cleaning back into the car just as his counterpart on the other side of the car put his mat back in.

Within thirty seconds, the two guys covering the front sections put their mats back in and all closed the doors. Next, each guy was responsible for washing his section of the car. They sudsed the car down and then stepped back as a fifth guy then hosed the car down.

Once all the suds were off, Travis's team stepped back over to the car and toweled it down until it was dry. Their last step in the process was to take window cleaner and clean the windows to a sparkling shine.

The head of the blue team inspected the inside and outside of the car. With a clipboard the guy checked boxes off to ensure that it was cleaned to Wash and Dash's satisfaction. The guy then held up two thumbs to the crew; then he drove it to the customer service area for the customer to retrieve the car.

Travis figured the guy was striving to one day take Andre's place as he emulated him with his two-thumbs-up gesture. Travis shook his head, breathing hard, as he looked at what he thought was a bit of a spectacle. Before Travis could catch his breath, his team headed toward the next car that was being pulled up to start the whole process again.

He did his best to keep up with the guys for the next two cars, but by the fourth car, Travis was spent. He was hot, sweating, and tired. But the rest of the team was rolling like a steam engine.

As the next couple of cars rolled in, Travis found himself cutting corners by only using the vacuum to pick up large particles that he saw instead of methodically sweeping the vacuum in rows as he'd been instructed to do. His cutting of corners caused him to fail inspection two times in a row, thus causing the area to have to be redone. Because the car was not cleaned within the guaranteed time, both of the customers received coupons for a free car wash on their next visit.

After his third failed inspection, Andre came out to the car with another guy in a purple shirt and pulled

Travis from the team. He pulled Travis into the office to talk. Travis was glad to have the break. He needed a bottle of cold water.

Andre must have been able to read Travis's mind because he pulled a bottle of cold water out of the refrigerator in his office.

"Travis, you look pretty hot and tired," Andre said.

Travis took long gulps of water. He'd never felt so thirsty in his life. His stomach didn't feel good and he was starting to feel a little dizzy. He sat in a seat in the office.

"You okay?" Andre asked.

"Yeah," Travis said, even though he did not feel well at all.

"Travis, my man, we've had a couple of customer complaints about the time it took for their cars to be cleaned. And we've had to give out three coupons today within a three-hour period."

Travis nodded his head, knowing that the coupons had been given out because of mistakes he'd made.

"Well, I gotta tell you, we normally only give out three coupons a week, at the max." Andre shook his head. "Man, at this rate, Wash and Dash store number 103 will go out of business in no time."

Travis knew exactly what was coming next: the ax.

"Man, I gotta let you go. Wash and Dash isn't for everyone and it looks like it isn't for you either." Andre, who looked like the hyena, wasn't laughing like one now.

Travis took another gulp of water. He set the bottle down on Andre's desk and gave him a two-thumbs-up sign. Then he jumped up and ran to the bathroom, where he threw up most of the water he'd drunk.

Andre was gracious enough to drive him home. After stepping out of the passenger side of the car, Travis looked back toward the window Andre had rolled down and thanked him.

"Thanks, Andre, for driving me home," Travis said.

"No problem, man. Are you sure you are going to be okay?" Andre asked with concern.

"Yeah, I think I just got a little dehydrated. I am going to head on in and take it easy as I try to get some fluids in me." He held up the second bottle of water Andre had given him. "I need to sip the water instead of gulping it down."

"Okay, well take it easy, man. And I am sorry I had to let you go, but you understand."

"Yeah, I understand. You take it easy too." Travis turned and headed up the driveway to the front door.

As soon as he got into the house, he set the bottle down on the counter in the kitchen and pulled out some grapes from the refrigerator. His stomach felt empty. He turned on the radio and started humming with the lyrics to the song "The Moment." And it only took him a moment to realize that he needed to be the ninth caller so he could win tickets to the Sonnette concert.

He had no idea if he was too late, but it was worth a try. He dialed the number to the radio station and it rang on the first try. Travis felt sure that someone had already probably been chosen as the ninth caller. When the DJ answered the call Travis was prepared to hear the words "Sorry, we already have a winner," but he didn't hear those words.

"Hello," he heard the DJ say.

"Ah, hello," Travis replied.

"Who am I speaking to?" the DJ asked.

"This is Travis."

"Travis," the DJ said.

"Yes," Travis said.

"Do you know what caller you are?"

"Uh, caller number nine?" Travis asked, thinking that he might be since the DJ was taking more than two seconds to talk to him.

"Yes, Travis, you are caller number nine," the DJ said, yelling into the microphone.

"Yes." Travis did his own yell into the phone.

"Do you know what you've won?" the DJ asked.

"Tickets to the Sonnette concert, right?"

"You are correct, Travis. Not only have you won front-row tickets to the show, you and a guest will get the VIP treatment and will be able to go backstage to meet Sonnette after the show."

"What? Are you serious?" Travis asked in disbelief.

"Yep."

"This is great. I've been trying to win tickets for weeks now," Travis said.

"Well, you can stop trying now and you can start getting ready for the show," the DJ said. "Travis, who is your favorite radio station for the hottest songs and hottest tickets?" the DJ asked.

"Foxy 107.1." Travis yelled this in the phone.

He heard music start to play on the radio. On the phone the DJ asked him to hold on for a moment. After a couple of seconds the DJ came back on to the phone and asked him his full name and address. He then told Travis when and where he could pick up his tickets for the show. Travis thanked him and hung up.

He'd almost forgotten about his job loss that day until his stomach started to ache again. Smiling, he picked up the bottle of water off of the counter and took a couple of sips as he thought about calling Tory to ask her if she would like to go to the Sonnette concert with him. Then he wondered if Tory would even appreciate the soulful songs that Sonnette sang. He'd hold off for a couple of days just in case another prospect came his way. He was going to have to remember that he was supposed to have a player state of mind.

Chapter 8

Travis decided not to job hunt, but instead took the day off, feeling he deserved a break from all the hard work he'd done the previous week. He felt a lot better after sipping water the rest of the evening before and eating some fruit. Andre had encouraged him to go to the hospital to make sure he hadn't gotten heatstroke, but Travis's pocket couldn't afford a trip to the emergency room. So he hoped and prayed that drinking the water and eating pieces of juicy fruit would help his condition, and gladly it had.

For the first part of the day he hung around the house watching TV, first watching a church service on television. He felt a little bad about not actually going to a church service, but then shrugged it off. Then he watched some episodes of *CSI* on the DVR.

That next day, Monday, he ventured out at lunch time to go the library to check his e-mail. After he left the e-mail he headed to Starbucks to get a cup of coffee. He had a coupon for a free cup of coffee with a Danish purchase.

He found a seat in the corner at a table. As he drank his coffee he people watched, observing people inside and outside of the store as they went about their daily lives. The Danish he'd chosen was tasty and the Starbucks coffee ended up being some of the best coffee he'd ever tasted, especially after he added the sugar, cream, and a sprinkle of cinnamon to it.

He almost choked on his coffee when he glanced toward the door and saw Jade Morris. She still looked as good as she had the first time he saw her at the Wash and Dash. Today she wore a tight-fitting business suit that hung on her perfectly. Her hair was pulled up in a bun and she wore a pair of glasses that made her look smart and very businesslike. She carried an attaché case and her purse. He figured that maybe she was on a break from her job and wondered if she worked somewhere nearby.

As the woman completed her transaction, getting her own cup of coffee, she made her way to the area to put sugar and cream into her cup. Travis thought about approaching her to say hello. He looked down at his clothing and suddenly wished he'd chosen something better to wear out instead of the jeans and T-shirt he'd chosen.

He hunched his shoulders and went for broke as he slid out of his booth to approach her.

"Hi, miss," Travis said as he walked up next to her.

She looked around to see if he was talking to her, and when she realized he was, she said, "Hello."

The hello was void of any warmth; it was more functional than anything else. It didn't look as if she recognized him at all from the car wash.

"You look familiar. I think I've seen you somewhere," Travis said.

She stirred the cream and sugar in her cup and said, "Oh really?"

"Yeah, I think I saw you at the Wash and Dash a couple weeks ago," Travis said.

Still Jade looked at him blankly. She did not remember that he was the one who had cleaned her car.

"Ah, yeah, I was getting the platinum service on my car." Travis had no idea why he'd just told that lie, but figured if he'd been truthful the woman would have given him a smirk and would have gone about her business.

For a second it looked as if a light went off in the woman's head, as she finally let a smile cross her lips. "The platinum service, huh? What kind of car do you have?"

Without a second of hesitation Travis said, "I have a BMW 135i, candy apple–red."

He had finally gotten the woman's attention. The platinum service was the most expensive service at the car wash. And now that she believed he had a BMW of his own, he figured the woman must have figured he must also have some money.

Travis continued talking. "Excuse my appearance; my office is being renovated and I decided to take the day off to run a few errands." Lies continued to flow out of his mouth.

She stuck her hand out for a handshake. "I'm Jade," she said.

Travis shook her hand. She had a very firm handshake. "You can call me Wayne," Travis said. This name flowed out of his mouth. He figured if he was going to present himself as something he wasn't, then he might as well take on the whole persona.

"Well, it is nice to meet you," Jade said. "Although, I have to admit, I don't remember ever seeing you at the Wash and Dash."

"It's okay. I believe you were sitting in the waiting area. I was outside making a few calls," Travis said.

Jade took a sip from her coffee to test it, then put the top on it.

"So I see you aren't wearing a ring. Are you unattached?" Travis boldly asked.

Surprisingly, Jade was very forthcoming with him. "I am unattached at the moment," she said.

"Oh, well, this must be my lucky day." Travis smiled.

"Must be." Jade matched his smile.

"I wonder how much luckier I can get."

Jade looked at him with her eyebrows rising in question. "And what is that supposed to mean?"

"I'll bet you like the finer things in life—fine dining, going to the opera, and traveling to exotic places. Am I right?"

"And your guess would be right," Jade confirmed.

"What about concerts?"

"That depends on who it is," Jade said.

"How about Sonnette?"

Jade's eyes widened. "You have tickets to see Sonnette next weekend?"

Trying to remain cool in his Wayne persona, Travis said, "I sure do. Front-row seats in fact."

She touched his forearm with a tap. "Are you serious? Those tickets have been sold out for weeks. I wanted to go but got the dates wrong, not realizing the concert was on Mother's Day. And by the time I checked, there were only nosebleed-section tickets." She wrinkled her nose and forehead.

"So would you like to go with me?"

Jade looked at him like he was joking. "Are you serious?"

"Yeah, I'm serious. This is my lucky day, remember?"

Jade let out a laugh and nodded her head. "You did say it was your lucky day." She looked down at her cup like she was contemplating.

"So what's up? Is it my lucky day or what?" Travis asked.

"Man, I don't even know you. How am I supposed to go out with a guy I don't even know?"

"Well you can get to know me, and if you don't go out with me, then you won't ever know me, will you?" Travis asked.

"You've got a point, but you are still a stranger. I mean you could be some kind of killer or something. I watch those movies on Lifetime."

This time Travis laughed. "I've seen a few of those movies on Lifetime too, but I assure you I am harmless."

Jade looked down at her watch again.

"It looks like you've got to be somewhere," Travis said.

"Yeah, I need to get back to work."

"So is it a yes or no?" Travis smiled. "It's my lucky day. Maybe we can make it your lucky day also."

Jade smiled back. "I tell you what; give me your phone number and I'll call you to let you know. Let me think about this first."

Travis frowned. "Okay, but don't keep a guy waiting."

"I won't." She smiled to reassure him. "Now what is your number?"

Travis gave her his phone number, which she put into her phone.

"Okay, Wayne. I'll call you to let you know what I've decided. And I promise I won't make you wait too long." She looked at her watch again.

"I'll let you go. I need to go run some errands myself." Travis led her to the door and opened it for her. She bid him good-bye and headed down the street. Travis headed in the other direction as if he had someplace he had to be. After a few steps he turned to see where Jade was. He saw her step into a building a block down. Then he slowed his pace.

He couldn't believe his luck that day. He'd actually run into Miss Jade Morris, and had the possibility of going out on a date with her.

Travis felt his cell phone vibrating in his pocket. He pulled it out, hoping it was Jade. It was a local Silvermont number. He stepped into a convenience store to get away from the noise from the street and then answered the phone. To his disappointment it wasn't Jade. It was someone calling him to do a survey.

He told the person on the phone that he was in the middle of something and couldn't talk. The peppy person told him she would try him another day and Travis gladly hung up.

While in the store he decided to buy a couple of lottery scratch-off tickets. He ended up buying five one-dollar tickets and one five-dollar ticket. As soon as he bought them he scratched them off right there in the store. He saw no need to go back to the house and scratch them off, especially if he won something.

After scratching off all the dollar tickets, Travis started feeling like he had just wasted ten dollars. The chance of him winning big was slim to just about none. When he scratched all the numbers off of the five-dollar ticket and looked to see if he had any matches, Travis grinned like the Cheshire cat.

On this particular scratch-off, he needed to match one of the four numbers at the top with one of the numbers at the bottom. One of his numbers matched. There was a thirty-seven at the top and one at the bottom. Just below the thirty-seven at the bottom, there was a $100 bill sign, which meant he had just won $100. It was his lucky day after all.

Chapter 9

The next few days seemed to pass by extremely slowly. Travis hadn't had any calls or e-mails with any new job offers. He'd mainly stayed around the house, exercising, eating, and looking at cable and movies.

He'd never thought there would be a day on which he'd be tired of taking it easy, but he was. With the house being void of any other life, there were times when he felt lonely. Calls to his uncle were never answered or returned. And the calls he'd intermittently gotten from Beryl he'd started listening to, to make sure there was nothing wrong with his sons, but he never called Beryl back.

It was now only two days away from the Sonnette concert and he still hadn't heard from Jade. Many times he'd contemplated asking Tory if she'd want to go to the concert, but he still held out hope that Jade would call. But now that the time was so near, he seriously doubted Jade would ever call. So he made up his mind to go ahead and call Tory to invite her to the concert instead.

He still didn't think that Tory would be all that into Sonnette's music, but at least he'd have someone there with him at the concert. He'd feel like a fool sitting in the front row of the concert by himself. He could have kicked himself for waiting so long for Jade in the first place. She probably forgot about him as soon as she stepped out of the door at Starbucks.

He dialed Tory's number.

"Well hello, stranger," Tory said with what sounded like a smile in her voice. Obviously she'd seen his name on the caller ID.

"Hello, Miss Tory," Travis said.

"T.J., what have you been up to? I thought you fell off the earth."

"Ah, nothing much. I've been busy looking for jobs," Travis said.

"Looking for a job?" Tory asked. He could hear concern in her voice.

"Ah, uh, yeah." He'd forgotten that he'd never told her he didn't have a job. "Yeah, I lost my job since I talked to you last. So I've been trying to focus on job hunting. That's why you haven't heard from me." Travis tried to clean up the story he was telling.

"Wow, I am sorry to hear that. What kind of work are you looking for?" Tory asked.

"At this point, something that will help me get back on my feet," Travis said in all truthfulness.

"If I hear of anything, I'll let you know."

"Thanks, Tory. That is sweet of you," Travis said.

"Just trying to help a good man out. I mean, you helped me once."

"I knew there was something I liked about you," Travis said. Tory was sweet and he wouldn't mind spending the night with her at the concert. "Hey, Tory."

"Yeah?"'

"What kind of . . ." Travis's voice trailed off as he heard his phone beep, indicating he had a call coming in on the other line.

"Yeah, Travis?"

"Hold on a second, Tory. I've got a call on the other line," Travis said.

"Sure."

Travis clicked over and said, "Hello?"

"Hello, may I speak to Wayne?"

Only one person would be calling asking to speak to a Wayne and that was Jade. Her voice sounded the same but a lot more sultry than he'd remembered it sounding the day he spoke to her in Starbucks.

"This is Wayne. With whom am I speaking?" Travis wanted to sound sophisticated and he also didn't want Jade to think he'd been sitting around waiting for her call.

"Wayne, you don't know my voice?"

"Let me guess, is this Jade?"

"Yeah, I'm hurt."

"No, you're not. I was just playing with you," Travis said.

Without beating around the bush, Jade said, "Is that invitation to go to the Sonnette concert still open?"

"Yeah," Travis said a little more quickly than he'd meant to say.

"Good. Sorry it took me so long to get back with you," Jade said.

"No worries," Travis said, glad he hadn't asked Tory. Then he remembered that he had Tory on hold on the other line. He contemplated asking Jade to hold for a moment, then decided against it for fear that he'd lose Jade on the line.

"Great," Jade said. "There's just one thing."

"What's that?" Travis asked.

"Since I still don't really know you, I'd like to meet you at the concert if that is okay with you."

Overall, it wasn't okay with Travis. But when he thought about it, he couldn't really object since he didn't have a car to take her to the concert in, and he didn't think it would be right to ask her to pick him up.

"Sure, I completely understand," Travis said. "I know how you women can get, being all cautious and all. We can meet there."

"Great," Jade said.

Travis gave her the details on when the concert was to start and they agreed on a time and place to meet outside of the concert. In his mind Travis still knew he needed to work out the logistics of how he was going to get from Silvermont to Durham to get to the concert himself.

"Okay, so I'll talk with you and see you the day after tomorrow," Jade said.

"So what if I need to call you before then or the day of the concert? Then what?"

"Just call me. My number came up on your caller ID, right?" Jade said as if it was an obvious fact.

"Yeah, I guess I could just save it," Travis said. He would have preferred that she had just given him the number. But he guessed getting it off the caller ID would have to work.

"Oooh, I am so excited," Jade said. "Now I've got to find something to wear."

Travis hadn't thought about what he was going to wear yet either.

"Thanks again, Wayne. See you the day after tomorrow," Jade said.

"Uh, okay. Well, the day after tomorrow it is then," Travis said, trying to sound cool with the way she was abruptly ending the call.

"Bye," Jade said.

"Bye," Travis said as he heard the click before he could get the word out good.

He didn't know how to react to the call: elated that she'd finally called, but dejected because she seemed more excited about seeing Sonnette than actually going with him and getting to know him better.

When he tried to click back over, Tory wasn't on the phone. Tory hadn't called back so he figured she'd probably gotten busy with something else herself. He would call her back later.

Right then he needed to focus on his date with Jade. He was finally going to get a chance to spend some time with the woman he'd admired from afar just a few short weeks ago. His daydreams might actually become a reality—that is, if he played the part right.

Looking through Brent's collection of movies, Travis found the one he was looking for. He put the *Pretty Woman* DVD into the DVD disc changer that sat on one of the recliners and watched the etiquette skills of Richard Gere to prepare for his date with Jade.

Sunday rolled around quickly. Travis looked through his clothing, trying to find something suitable for his date with Jade. He could have kicked himself for waiting until the last minute to put an outfit together. The event was to be held at the Durham Performing Arts Center, also known as the DPAC. The DPAC was located in downtown Durham, North Carolina.

He wanted to be dressed to the nines to impress Jade. And after over an hour of looking for something suitable, he came to the realization that none of his clothing would pass as anything dressy enough for the concert.

The concert would start in just seven hours. Travis sat on the side of his bed and pondered his dilemma. He thought about how nice it would be to have a nice suit to wear. But he knew that buying a suit would cost

him a little more than he had received from his last
check at the car wash. He still had fifty dollars from the
money he'd won on the lottery scratch-off but it was in
an envelope in a drawer. The envelope he put the fifty
dollars in was for the money he was attempting to save.
Fifty dollars wasn't a lot, but it was a start.

A suit would set him back. He even thought that a
nice shirt and a nice pair of slacks would work, but
those two items would cost also. Even if he did get an
outfit, then he'd need shoes to go with the clothing.

This was indeed a time when he wished he could borrow an outfit from a cousin, friend, or even his Uncle
Billy across town. He and Billy were about the same
stature and build. But not only was Billy all the way
across town, he hadn't answered any of Travis's recent
phone calls.

Then, like a light switch turning on a light bulb in his
head, Travis realized he did have a friend from whom
he could borrow some clothing. He and Brent were the
same size and build as well. He made a beeline straight
to Brent's bedroom and closet.

When he opened Brent's closet, Travis thought he'd
died and gone to clothing heaven. The closet was neat
and the clothing seemed to be organized in categories. There was a section for jeans, casual shirts, dress
shirts, dress slacks, suits. Many of the items still had
price tags on them. In the corner of the closet, there
was even a double-breasted Armani tuxedo.

One wall of the closet had been designated for shoes.
The wall had cubbies made especially for Brent's shoes
and even those were categorized by style and color.
From the looks of the amount of clothing in the closet,
it didn't look as if Brent had taken any clothing, but
there were a few shoe cubbies that were missing pairs
of shoes.

For a few moments, Travis just stood in the center of the closet. He turned around and around in awe with his mouth slightly agape. He wished that he could one day have a closet like this one filled with nice clothing.

He took a deep breath. His clothing worries had just been eliminated. Behind the door of Brent's closet, Travis found a full-length mirror. Acting as if he were America's next top male model, he tried on outfit after outfit and checked himself out in the mirror.

After almost an hour of trying on clothing, he found what he thought was the perfect concert outfit. Once he slipped on a pair of Brent's Cole Haan shoes, like Cinderella with the prince slipping the shoe on her foot, Brent's shoe fit Travis like a glove. The outfit was complete.

Chapter 10

For the second time in his life, Travis felt as if he could grace the pages of *GQ* magazine. The first time was when he donned his tuxedo at his wedding and the second time was right then as he stood outside of the Durham Performing Arts Center.

He patiently waited for Jade outside of the DPAC. He felt confident because he knew he looked and smelled good. Like a child in a candy store, Travis had looked at the multiple bottles of cologne Brent had. He'd sniffed a few bottles and finally decided on the Old Spice.

And just before leaving the house to get into his taxi, he'd splashed on some Old Spice cologne. He had to chuckle when he did, as he thought about the Old Spice commercials with the actor with the deep voice, various backgrounds, and sound effects while he talked about the cologne.

With only a few minutes to spare before the concert was to begin, Jade strode up looking fabulous in a tight-fitting purple dress with a lavender shawl over her arms and a matching purse clutched under her arm. On her feet she wore stiletto heels and Travis wondered how in the world she'd walked all the way from the parking deck in the shoes. Her hair and nails looked as if she had just come from the salon.

When she saw him a smile spread across her face. When she finally met up with him she gave him a light peck on his cheek. "I am so sorry I am late. I meant to be here on time, but you know how hairdressers can be."

Travis looked at the clock on his cell phone. "We'd better go ahead and get on in there," he said.

As they walked Travis said, "How in the world did you walk all the way from the parking deck in those shoes?"

"Oh, I didn't walk from the deck."

"Yeah, but the parking on the street isn't really that close either," Travis said.

"Oh no, honey, I parked in the VIP section. A friend of mine works the shows here sometimes and told me he could get me in there."

Travis wondered why she hadn't told him about the friend and offered the hookup in the VIP section. Although he had to admit that even if she had, it wasn't like he had a car of his own anyway. But it was still the principle of the thing. She still could have offered, whether he was a stranger or not. She had accepted his invitation to come to the concert with him.

The fact that she was late and didn't have the common courtesy to offer him the information about the VIP parking perturbed him. This was along with the fact that he'd spend thirty dollars for a taxi to get to the concert and would be spending the same amount after the concert was over to get back home.

Once they got in and settled in their seats, the rest of the night during the concert went well. Jade knew the words to most of the songs, and stood for much of the concert as she sang songs right along with Sonnette. At one point the singer looked directly at Travis and Jade as she sang one of her famous songs about couples in love. And even though they were not a couple, and much less in love, it was nice to have Sonnette's attention for a brief moment. And that attention made Jade enjoy the concert even more.

When the concert was over, Travis told Jade that they were going to be able to go backstage to meet Sonnette. Jade was thrilled, but the thrill turned into disappointment when she realized that they were not the only couple to go backstage to meet Sonnette. Travis and Jade had been herded to the back with ten other couples. As if they were in factory mode, they took a quick picture with Sonnette and also received a pre-signed photo of the songstress.

Realizing that it looked as if they were a real couple and were only going to get one signed photograph, Travis asked for another. That way he would ensure that they would both have the souvenir to take home.

Once they were back outside after the concert, Jade again gave him a peck on the cheek similar to the one she had greeted him with a few hours before. Then she yawned, saying she was tired and needed to go head home. Travis got the message loud and clear that she didn't feel like hanging out to grab something to eat, or see what else they might be able to get into that night. Again, he was a bit perturbed, but it didn't last very long since with another thirty-dollar fare to get back home, his pockets really couldn't afford to do much else.

"Well, you've got my number, give me a call some time," Jade said.

"Ah, yeah, I'll do that," Travis said.

"Wayne, I really did have a good time. We'll have to see about meeting so maybe I can get to know you better," Jade said.

"Ah, yeah," Travis said. He gave her an awkward hug and said good-bye. He shook his head as he walked toward the parking deck, as if he was really parked there. He wondered if Jade had any home training, was an aloof person, or she was just trying to give him the cold shoulder? He figured maybe she was just an aloof person.

She hadn't formally given him her phone number. What if he'd erased his call log on the phone? Had she just assumed he'd kept the number? At that point he was unsure if he'd pick up the phone to call her. But then he thought about the tight dress she had on and quickly reconsidered. The girl looked good, and maybe it was just an off night for her.

By the time Travis did arrive home he was way too exhausted to sleep in his own bedroom, and he really didn't want to sleep on the couch or the recliner in the bonus room. So he opted for the only other viable option. He took a shower and crawled into Brent's king-sized bed.

That Tuesday morning Travis awoke to the sound of his cell phone's ring tone beat. As he opened his eyes and looked around the bedroom, he was confused as to where he was. Then he remembered that he'd fallen asleep in his friend Brent's room instead of the guest room that he was supposed to be in. He didn't want to get up out of the warm, soft bed. Travis didn't know what kind of sheets Brent had bought, but he was going to have to find out the name brand because he had never slept on sheets so smooth and comfortable in his life.

Seeing it was Tory calling he answered the phone. He felt bad for not calling her back the other night.

"Hello," Travis said.

"Hey, T.J. What's up? I haven't heard from you in a couple of days."

"I know, something came up and I had to handle it. Sorry I didn't call you back the other day."

"Don't worry about it. I know you have a lot on your mind. How is the job search going?"

"It's going nowhere," Travis said, not wanting to keep up false pretenses about his job search with Tory.

"I really hate to hear that. And I can tell it is really getting you down by the way you sound. Is there anything I can do?" Tory asked. She sounded so very sweet and genuine.

"Nah, not unless you know someone hiring right now," Travis said.

"I wish I did."

Travis sat up in the bed and looked over at the clock on Brent's nightstand. It was already 11:00; he couldn't believe he'd slept so long.

"I was calling to invite you to go out with me and my friends this evening. We're going bowling. And don't worry about paying, it will be my treat," Tory said.

Travis thought about it. And he guessed he must have paused too long as he thought about it, because Tory started talking again.

"Come on, I can hear the moping in your voice. Come on and meet me so you can take your mind off of things for a little while."

Travis's mind hadn't really been that pressed about the job situation, but he guessed it must have sounded that way since he was still a bit groggy from just waking up. He thought it might actually be good for him to get out of the house.

"Sure, sounds good," Travis said.

"We are meeting at the bowling center on Third Street at two o'clock," Tory informed him.

Travis agreed that he would meet her at the bowling alley at 2:00. After taking a shower, he picked a pair of jeans and a T-shirt out of the pile of clothing on his bed. He did so without much thinking about how the outfit would look. The picking out of the clothing coupled with the ironing took only about five minutes versus his hour-long quest for the right outfit the night before.

He wasn't too concerned about how Tory perceived him, unlike with Jade. Tory had seen him at his most comfortable that first day, and she had even seen him during one of his most embarrassing moments when he took his dive at the skating rink. It was easy with Tory. He didn't have to put up any false pretenses. It was refreshing to just be himself.

That afternoon Travis hung out with Tory and her friends. And true to her word she paid for his games, bowling shoes, and even his snack. He had fun with Tory, who really liked to have a good time. She was easygoing and didn't mind laughing at herself and others. Travis was grateful for her act of kindness.

He was so grateful for her act of kindness and was enjoying her company so much that he decided to ask her if she would like to go to the movies with him after bowling. Tory agreed and they headed over to the two-dollar movie theater that was just a couple of blocks from the bowling alley.

At the theater, Travis sprang for both of their movie tickets, a tub of refillable popcorn, and their drinks, even though Tory insisted he didn't have to pay for her. In all he'd spent less than twenty dollars. And he inwardly shook his head thinking that he would have probably gotten off a lot cheaper the night before if he'd gone ahead and invited Tory to the concert instead of Jade. Plus Tory probably wouldn't have minded picking him up and dropping him back off at home.

Tory picked a movie Travis had already seen a couple of times. But he didn't mind seeing it again with her. He liked watching how she reacted to the funny scenes as well as the parts that were meant to be tearjerkers. She laughed and teared up at all the right spots.

With Tory, Travis felt alive and in control. In their conversations, she looked to him for advice about some of the smallest of things, like how to roll the bowling ball down the alley and what he thought about the differences in the various grades of gas to put in the car. He'd been able to easily help her with the answers to those questions and many others as they chatted while walking and waiting for the movie to begin.

Unlike Jade the night before, Travis could tell Tory was having a good time with him, not just having a good time with the activities they were partaking in. Once the movie was over, Travis didn't want their time together to end. He didn't look forward to going home to an empty house, so he asked her if she wanted to catch another movie. She agreed and this time they watched an action and suspense movie.

The second movie was one Travis hadn't seen, and they were both enthralled in the plot of the movie together. Tory had a tendency to talk out loud while watching the movie, and while it hadn't bothered him with the first movie, because he'd seen it before, it did bother him with the second movie.

He tried to give her a hint by not responding to her comments and not turning his head to make eye contact, but she just seemed oblivious to the fact that she was bothering him. One of his biggest pet peeves was for someone to talk through a movie. About halfway through, he resigned himself to the fact that Tory wasn't going to be quiet. He'd have to come back another day alone and check it out.

At the movie's end, Travis was tired. Tory, on the other hand, wanted to hang out longer and had suggested their going out to a nightclub. She was like the

Energizer Bunny and wanted to keep going and going and going.

When they stepped outside of the theatre, Tory pulled a package out of her purse. It was a package of cigarettes. Then she pulled out a cigarette lighter and lit the cigarette. Travis's stomach turned, not literally but figuratively. He had dated a smoker only once before in his life and kissing her wasn't pleasant. He didn't want to think about kissing Tory now, not that he had up until that moment. Travis realized he saw Tory as what she was, a young lady who was seven years his junior, not as a sexual object. But, nonetheless, she was definitely fun to be around. He would just have to take her in spells.

He knew that if he was going to continue to hang around Tory, then he was going to have to keep up some type of exercise routine. He was also going to have to make a list of things to buy. On the top of that list would be a bottle of multivitamins.

Chapter 11

Once Travis got back into the house after his date with Tory he checked his cell phone for messages. He'd put the phone on complete silence. He didn't know why, but he hoped Jade had called.

There weren't any missed calls or messages from Jade, but there were two missed calls from Beryl and one voice mail from her as well. He listened to the message, and as usual she was calling about money.

Talking with Beryl was draining. All she did was nag him about money, and she always wanted to tell him what he needed to be doing, and he was sick of it. It was as if her mission in life was to continuously remind him of what a failure he was as an ex-husband and as a father to his two boys. He just couldn't do anything right in her eyes. Her nagging attitude was one of the main reasons he wanted to move away in the first place.

Guilt got the best of him. Travis checked his wallet and pulled out seventy-five dollars. He found an envelope in Brent's office and addressed it to Beryl. Then he went out to the mailbox, and put the flag up on the box so the mailman would pick it up. Travis knew that seventy-five dollars wasn't a lot of money, but at the time it was all he was going to be able to do.

He missed Cameron, who was five years old, and Jayden, who was three years old, and wanted to see them, but felt like the hassle of going through his ex-wife was too much. At some point he knew he would

have to pick up the phone and call her, but it would
have to be on a day when he had a full stomach and a
restful night of sleep.

The popcorn he had eaten with Tory seemed to have
dissipated in his stomach. His stomach growled, an
indication he needed more food. So he pulled out a
frozen dinner and heated it in the microwave. As he
waited for the dinner to cook, he turned on the radio.

He heard an old church song that reminded him of
his dearly departed mother. He also missed church. Off
and on he watched church services on the television,
but had not actually stepped into a church in months.

There was one pastor in particular that he liked to
watch on Sunday mornings. The church, called New
Hope, was actually located right there in Silvermont,
and he'd contemplated attending a service one morning. As he listened to the song, he made it up in his
mind that in the morning he would make a trip to New
Hope Church and attend one of their services.

That Sunday morning Travis awoke bright and early.
The birds outside chirped a melodious song as if will-
ing him to come out and greet the day. And, like the
night before, Travis again turned on the radio to listen
to more gospel music. Listening to the music reminded
him of the days of his childhood when his mother
played spirituals on a Sunday morning just before Sunday School and church.

Beryl too had played gospel songs on Sunday mornings while getting ready for church. In many ways he
supposed Beryl's aura was very similar to his mother's
aura. And he figured Beryl's spirit was part of what
drew him to her in the first place.

His mother played the music as she cooked breakfast
for them, usually country ham, homemade biscuits,
eggs, and grits running with butter. Travis nodded his

head. He sure wished he had some of his mother's cooking right then. Subconsciously he rubbed his stomach. There wasn't any breakfast food in the refrigerator.

After taking his shower, he returned to his friend's closet to shop for more clothing to wear for church. He found a nice suit and tie along with a pair of matching shoes. Again he stood before the mirror and admired himself in the clothing. He now looked on the outside the way he felt on the inside.

He looked through one of the boxes of books he'd packed and found his Bible. With his hand he literally dusted if off and read the embossed gold inscription on the cover that said: TRAVIS W. HIGHGATE. It had been a present to him for his thirty-third birthday from Beryl.

Now that he was all dressed up and ready to go, he felt an inexplicable need to get to the church. He now hungered to hear the Word of God. Although his stomach grumbled, it wasn't edible food he yearned for, it was spiritual food he needed. With his Bible clutched in one hand, Travis then grabbed his wallet and keys and headed out to catch the bus to New Hope Church.

Travis stepped into the sanctuary of New Hope Church and immediately got the surprise of his life. Among the people in the pulpit of the church who were singing and clapping with the choir as they sang songs of praise, there stood his friend Phillip Tomlinson. Travis couldn't believe his eyes. Phillip was sitting front and center in the seat that was normally designated as the pastor's chair.

He racked his brain trying to remember if Phillip and his wife, Shelby, had ever said what church they went to. And as he thought about it he did recall that the couple was from Silvermont.

Travis quickly found a seat and opened up his program. The program listed Phillip as being one of the

ministers in the church filling in for the pastor. His
friend—well, really acquaintance—Phillip was the one
who would be delivering the sermon for the 8:30 and
11:00 A.M. services.

Phillip wasn't Travis's friend per se. He and Beryl
had met Phillip and Shelby while attending a marriage
retreat in the mountains of North Carolina. He and
Beryl had gone to the retreat in hopes of making their
marriage stronger. Phillip had been the minister facili-
tating the retreat.

Phillip knew much about his marriage to Beryl and
the problems they had. Phillip and the others at the
retreat actually knew more about his marriage than
Travis was comfortable with. And Travis knew a few
things about Phillip and Shelby. So even though Travis
couldn't really say they were friends or buddies, the
two men were on a first-name basis.

As the service began, Travis stood and clapped his
hands with the choir, eager to soon hear the Word of
God. From what he remembered, Phillip had a great
deal of insight, and even though he didn't want to admit it at the time, Phillip had even had insight on how
Travis's marriage would turn out when he didn't want
to hear what the man had to say—and he would pay attention this time.

In the same manner he'd used at the marriage retreat in the mountains, Phillip ministered and taught
the congregation of people. Travis wished he had
brought a pen with him so he could have jotted down
key points in the sermon with their corresponding
scriptures. In the end, the sermon had been too brief
for him. He wanted more of the Word. And even after
the benediction was over, Travis continued to sit in his
seat wishing he could hear more.

Then it dawned on him that he really didn't have any place in particular to be, so nothing was holding him back from staying for the next service. His stomach started to rumble and he remembered that it was empty. He looked at his watch and figured he would have just enough time to run over to the gas station that was adjacent to the parking lot of the church and grab a bite of something to eat—just enough to appease his stomach for the next couple of hours.

By the time he returned from the store to the church, it was almost filled to capacity. His stomach was coated with honey-roasted peanuts and orange juice. Determined not to sit in the back of the church, he ignored the ushers as they tried to point him to the back. Instead he headed toward the front of the church, sure there might be at least one or two vacant seats dispersed throughout.

To his luck he found a seat in the second row, front and center of the pulpit. Once seated he felt close enough to almost be able to touch Phillip, or to at least be able to possibly speak to him after the service was over.

As the service started for the second time with the choir singing the same songs they'd sung for the first service, Travis had a feeling of déjà vu. This time he clapped with more enthusiasm with the songs, as he now knew some of the words to the songs. The spirit was indeed alive in this church as the congregation praised the Lord as if all on one spiritual accord.

Travis had been to many a church service and had heard choirs sing and church members clap along with the beat of the music. But what he was experiencing right then at the second service was unlike anything he had ever experienced before. And he didn't know why he thought about it, but he knew this was the

kind of service his wife, Beryl, would thoroughly enjoy. He mentally caught himself. Beryl wasn't his wife
anymore. She was his ex-wife. That was the way she
wanted it and Travis would just have to adjust to that
fact and continue to move on with his life.

As Phillip preached along the same track he'd preached
in the previous service, Travis found himself whispering the Bible scriptures Phillip was going to say before
he said them. He'd also found himself whispering the
key points Phillip was about to say before he said them,
too. He jotted down notes in his newly purchased one-
subject notebook he'd gotten from the gas station. The
gas station attendant had given him a pen with the gas
station's logo on it.

A few times as he whispered words and statements he
remembered from the first service, Travis noticed the
woman sitting next to him glancing at him. He hoped
he wasn't being annoying by distracting her from the
service. So from then on he tried his best not to speak
aloud. Instead he mouthed the words.

After the second service he made a point to make
eye contact with the woman with an apologetic smile.
It felt good to smile and show his teeth without feeling
ashamed of them. In return the woman smiled back.

"Sorry if I was disturbing you during service," Travis
said. He stuck his hand out to her. "Hi, my name is
Travis."

She gave him a strong handshake. "Marla," she replied.

"I didn't mean to distract you," Travis said.

"You didn't disturb me," Marla said. "I was just admiring how much you know your Word."

"Oh, that," Travis said. "That was nothing—" Travis
started to say more about it being his second service
that morning, but Marla cut him off.

"You said it is Travis, right?" Marla asked.

"Yeah," Travis said. His eyebrows rose in question.

"Don't ignore the obvious gift the Lord has given you. You have insight into the Word and you shouldn't sell yourself short," Marla said. "The Lord gives us gifts and talents and it looks as if you have the gift of knowledge. You know the Word. It is evident. So don't run from your gift, embrace it."

Travis was speechless. He was taken aback. He had retained much of the information from the first service and found himself whispering the words Phillip was about to say from memory. And this woman actually thought he was speaking from self-knowledge or by some sort of gift from God. He was about to try to explain and correct her but she started talking again.

"I have to say that I admire a strong man of God and I see that in you," Marla said. "Are you a minister?"

"No," Travis said.

"Well I shouldn't stereotype, but you sure look like a preacher." She looked him up and down. Then she smiled. "Please excuse me for being so forward."

"No, miss, you are not being too forward. I'll take a compliment. I mean it's not like you told me I look like a bum or a pimp or anything."

Marla had a light brown skin complexion. And upon hearing Travis's comment her cheeks started to turn red. "Oh my goodness. I must sound like a complete fool."

"Nah, miss. I like the compliments. Keep them coming," Travis said. "It is miss, right?" Travis wanted to check and make sure he wasn't about to flirt with a married woman.

"It is. I am divorced." She took a deep breath. "Okay, let me try to redeem myself. I just thought you were a very nice-looking gentleman and I wanted to let you know."

"Well I am flattered. And thanks," Travis said.

Out of the corner of his eye he saw Phillip walking and talking with a few people as he attempted to leave the sanctuary. Travis tried to get Phillip's attention by waving at him. As he did, the woman touched his arm lightly and said that she had to leave and that maybe she'd see him again another Sunday.

By the time Travis realized he wasn't going to be able to get Phillip's attention the woman was going through the front doors of the church to exit. She seemed pretty nice and he had enjoyed the compliments she'd given him.

When he looked down to retrieve his Bible and notebook from his seat he saw that the woman had left her Bible in her seat. He headed to the foyer of the church and then out to the parking lot but didn't see any sign of her. So he figured he'd just hang on to the Bible. He could look for her the next Sunday and return it to her.

As he left the church, hailed the bus, and rode back to the house, Travis marveled about the fact that the woman had truly thought he was not only a man of God but she actually thought he was a minister. This thought actually blew his mind. Not that he was a heathen or anything, but he still had a way to go in the spiritual and ministering department. His first step would be to start going to church more often. So he vowed to himself that he would do just that. Next Sunday he would return to New Hope again.

Chapter 12

Weeks passed before Travis secured another job. It was the Friday before Father's Day and he would be starting his first day at a place called Alley's Pizza. Alley's was a kid-friendly restaurant with a play zone for kids to enjoy. The place put him in the mind of a Chuck E. Cheese's restaurant, except in addition to the little games the children could play to redeem tickets for prizes, they also had the gigantic jumping toys where kids could climb, jump, run, and slide until their hearts were content. Alley's had party rooms for special occasions like birthdays.

Travis's job was to be Alley the Alligator. At various intervals, Travis had to walk through the establishment and greet the customers. He also had to make appearances in each one of the birthday rooms to greet the happy little birthday boy or girl who was being honored for their special occasion.

He was told that the establishment was geared toward children between the ages of two and ten. He wasn't too keen on having to wear the alligator suit, but was glad that no one would know who he was underneath the protruding felt, shaped teeth.

Travis donned his alligator suit and felt foolish. Each step he took was awkward and he had to be careful when he walked because of his big, bulky feet. For the first two hours he waddled from room to room greeting children for parties, and standing outside in front of the store to try to entice more people to come in and check Alley's out.

A couple of times he had to shake a couple of children off of his tail as they wanted to try to climb onto it and ride. Although he didn't like wearing the alligator suit, he did like the fact that the head of the alligator muffled the sounds of the screaming and shrieking children. And as the hours ticked on, he really didn't know how long he was going to be able to play the role of Alley.

Just as he was about to step into the dinosaur birthday room to greet a little boy who was turning five years old, Travis thought he saw a woman who favored Beryl, but this woman had a short haircut, unlike his ex-wife who had beautiful flowing dreads. He'd done a double take, but when he did, whoever the woman was had gotten lost among a crowd of people who were coming in the front door. He figured the heavy suit with its claustrophobic feel was finally getting to him.

After greeting the little boy in the dinosaur room, Travis made a round around the perimeter of the big play area, while the manager played the theme song for Alley's, which went to the same beat as the song "Twinkle, Twinkle, Little Star": "Come on, kids, follow Alley. Jump and play and eat, yippee." The deal was that Travis was to do a walking dance around the perimeter while the children danced and walked behind him with a conga-line type of feel. Once he'd gone around the perimeter two times the music would end and the children could go back to playing.

As Travis walked back toward the break room, he did another double take. On the giant dragon, he thought he saw a little boy who looked just like his youngest son Jayden. Then a moment later he stared at another boy and knew for sure it was his oldest son Cameron.

He blinked his eyes and wondered what was going on. It was surreal seeing his boys there. He wanted to pinch himself but couldn't because of all of the padding he was wearing. The boys sat at the top of the slide on the dragon.

He looked about, knowing Beryl would never let the boys go too far out of her sight. He turned his suit-clad body around, almost knocking a child over with his tail. He bent over to make sure the child was okay and then continued looking around. That was when he saw Beryl smiling up toward the boys, encouraging them to slide down. She looked the same but very different: she had cut all of her dreads off and was now sporting a short haircut, which didn't look bad with her oval-shaped face.

His first thought was to try to duck out of sight so that Beryl would not see him. Then he wondered how she might have found out he worked there. He realized there was no way she would recognize him in the alligator suit, and besides that, she was watching the boys play as if she didn't have a care in the world. So it was clear that she was there on her own and not seeking him.

As he stood there watching Beryl, who was oblivious to the fact that Alley the Alligator was staring at her, Travis saw a tall, skinny-looking guy who reminded him of Urkel from the old *Family Matters* television show. This Urkel lookalike didn't wear any glasses.

The guy walked up to Beryl, handed her an ICEE drink, and then put his arm around Beryl's waist. Beryl took the drink and placed her arm around the guy as well as if they were a couple.

Travis's jaw dropped wide open. "What the . . ." His voice trailed off as he was tapped from behind.

"Hey, T, we've been waiting on you. You've got to go to the princess birthday room to make an appearance," Travis's new boss said. The boss called him T because there was already another Travis who worked there, and it made things simpler for everyone to distinguish who was who.

With reluctance Travis followed his boss to the princess-themed room. In the room he danced the Alley the Alligator dance and sang "Happy Birthday" to the little girl, who turned out to be afraid of him the whole time he was in there. In Travis's mind he and the little girl had something in common: she didn't want him to be there and he didn't want to be in there either. As soon as was humanly possible he'd hightail it out of the room to seek out his ex-wife and her friend, whoever he was.

This time when he found them the guy didn't have his arm around Beryl but he was whispering something into her ear. Whatever he said she must have liked because she started giggling as she hit the guy playfully on his arm. The guy smiled like he'd just scored a point in a game.

Travis felt himself getting hot, and not because of the heavy suit he was wearing. What was that man doing whispering sweet nothings into his sons' mother's ear? And the guy had the nerve to do it right in front of his kids. The next thing he knew his baby boy, Jayden, ran up to the guy. The guy scooped his son up and swung him around in the air. Travis's youngest son giggled with glee. The guy put him back down on the floor, so he could go back and play with his big brother.

Before Travis knew it his body was off in a forward-moving, wobbling run headed toward his ex and the guy. Just before reaching them he tripped over his two oversized alligator feet and fell into the guy, causing the bright red ICEE drink he was holding to fly into his face and down to the Urkel lookalike's sky-blue Polo shirt and the white linen shorts he was wearing.

Just as Travis picked himself up off of the floor, the guy pushed him, asking what his problem was. Travis pushed the guy back and a fight ensued. Neither man received any bruises during the tangle due to the fact that Travis suit was well cushioned and because Travis's big alligator hands were soft and could only throw soft blows.

The manager had to end up coming over to pull the two men apart. Before Travis could say a word the guy started telling the manager what happened. Travis tried to catch his breath in the meantime. He was seething within.

Travis's manager looked at the whole mess. "T, go to the office. We'll talk in a few minutes.

Travis was about to say something. He wasn't going leave without telling his side of the story. But then he realized the place was quiet. As he looked around, people watched, trying to see what would happen next. Then he ended up keeping his mouth shut when he saw his two little boys hugging their mother with tears in their eyes. Travis realized what a complete spectacle it must have all been. And now his two little boys were seemingly terrified of the big bully alligator.

With newfound humiliation because of his actions, Travis turned to go to the locker area so he could take the slushy, stained alligator suit off. As he walked away he heard his boss apologizing profusely to the guy he'd just fought. As he passed them, children shied away and he received glares from the adults.

As he wobbled past the princess party room, the little girl from the party he had recently visited screamed to the top of her lungs as she cried, "Alley's hurt. Blood, Daddy, blood."

Now Travis really couldn't wait to get out of the outfit and couldn't get out of the place fast enough.

Chapter 13

The Sunday of Father's Day Travis sat in silence in the recliner of the bonus room. He'd tried to concentrate at church that morning and then later tried to watch a movie when he got back home, but kept having to rewind it because it wasn't keeping his attention. Father's Day came and went without a phone call from Beryl or the boys.

That night he tossed and turned as his thoughts kept wondering why in the world Beryl had been in Silvermont. It was true that Silvermont was less than two hours from where they used to live. But she hadn't usually frequented Silvermont. Greensboro or even Raleigh, but not Silvermont. What was she doing there on a weekday, no less?

By Monday Travis had had enough of stewing over everything and trying to figure out what Beryl was doing in Silvermont as well as who the Urkel-looking guy was. He picked up the phone and did something he hadn't done in months: he dialed Beryl's cell phone number ready to give her the third degree with the barrage of questions he had swirling in his head.

As soon as he heard Beryl's voice say hello, he asked, "Who was that guy you were with at Alley's the other day?" His voice was louder than he had intended for it to be. He'd intended to ask her more, but realized he'd actually gotten her voice mail. She'd changed her message since the last time he'd spoken with her and her pause just after saying, "Hello," on the message made it seem like she was actually answering the phone.

When the phone did finally beep for him to leave his message, he hung up instead. He didn't want to give her a heads-up on why he was calling. He wanted her honest reaction and response to the questions he had. So next he dialed her number at work. He knew Beryl didn't like to be disturbed at work, but this was one time she was going to have to make an exception. He had questions that needed to be answered right then. After punching in her direct extension from memory, he again poised himself to ask the questions.

"Hello," a woman's voice said.

Travis's words stuck in his throat for a moment. It wasn't Beryl's voice.

"Hello," the woman said again.

"Ah, yes. Who am I speaking with?"

"Oh, I'm sorry. I'm Betsy. I was supposed to say my name when I answered. Please forgive me. How can I help you, sir?"

"Uh, yes, may I please speak with Beryl Highgate?"

"Beryl Highgate?" The woman repeated in question.

"Yes, Beryl Highgate," Travis repeated.

"Oh, that's how her name is pronounced," Betsy said.

Beryl's name was pronounced just like the name Cheryl but with a B. Travis didn't feel like talking with the woman and didn't feel like going through all the formalities and niceties. "Look, Betsy, I am in a bit of a rush. Is Beryl available or not?"

There was a pause on the other end. It was obvious that the woman had been offended. "Well, sir, I am sorry but Ms. Highgate is not available. She no longer works here."

"Say what?" Travis asked in disbelief.

"She no longer works here, sir. Now is there anything I can help you with, sir?" The woman sounded snippy now.

"No," Travis said.

He guessed Betsy was tired of being customer service friendly as well because the next thing he heard was a click in his ear. Now he sort of wished he'd been at least a little more cordial to the woman, because now he couldn't ask her any questions about where Beryl was and what happened for her not to be there anymore.

Travis sat dumbfounded for a moment, wondering what was going on. Beryl had worked at that office for almost a decade. She was a dedicated employee who had been employee of the month several times and employee of the year once. Now new questions formulated in his mind. Beryl no longer worked there? He wondered what was up. Had they had layoffs? Did she quit? How was she getting along financially without any support from him?

There were many times when they were married that Beryl used to nag him about working and keeping a job. It was hard for him to find steady work. He often applied for jobs but the people hiring didn't appreciate his associate's degree in general studies. At that time it had been hard enough for their family to make ends meet on Beryl's steady income.

Now he felt a twinge of guilt. He wondered if Beryl had been calling him so much the last few months because of her job loss. She probably really did need some money.

His cell phone rang, and without looking at the caller ID, he picked it up hoping to hear Beryl's voice. Instead of hearing his ex-wife, he heard the sultry voice of Jade on the other end.

"Hello, may I speak to Wayne?" Jade said.

"Hey, Jade," Travis said. Even though he was disappointed it wasn't Beryl, Jade was a pleasant distraction.

"Well hello, handsome," Jade said. Her voice held a seductive tone.

"Well hello to you too, stranger," Travis said. He wondered what Jade was up to and why she was calling and trying to sound so seductive.

"I am so sorry I haven't made contact with you. Things have just been really busy for me at work and there were a few personal things I had to take care of. So pleeeaaassse forgive me." She'd held out her please a little longer than needed to stress her need for forgiveness.

"You are forgiven," Travis said, now sort of glad she had called to take his mind off of the situation with his ex-wife. "So to what do I owe the pleasure of this call?"

"Well, I was wondering if you were going to be busy this Friday," Jade said.

"Well that depends. What's up?" Travis asked.

"There is a dinner party for my job that I completely forgot about until yesterday and I need to take a date with me. You immediately came to mind," Jade said.

"Are you serious? I am the first person who came to mind?"

"You sure were."

Travis didn't believe the woman. She was so good looking that she would surely have her pick of many men. So she either asked a few other people and they had declined or her original date had to back out at the last minute. But all was well and good.

"Where is this dinner and when?" Travis asked.

"It is at Ginny's this Friday, the twenty-fourth, at seven," Jade said.

"It's at Ginny's?" Travis asked, thinking that it sounded like it should be a nice dinner party and that whatever company Jade worked for, they had a lot of money.

"Yeah, Ginny's. Have you been there before?"

"Oh, yeah. It's my favorite restaurant. I love their food."

"Great. So how about it? Can you make it?"

"Sure," Travis said.

"Oh yeah, and Wayne," Jade said.

"Yeah?" Travis asked with question in his voice.

"There is one more little thing," Jade said.

"What's that?" Travis wondered.

"It is a formal affair. Do you happen to own a tuxedo?"

"Baby doll, are you serious?" Travis asked.

"Ah, yes," Jade said with what sounded like concern in her voice.

"Only real men own tuxedos," Travis said.

He could hear what sounded like a sigh of relief in her voice. "Great. I knew you looked like a man who would own your own tuxedo. Wonderful. You can pick me up at six," Jade said.

"Ah, say what?"

"You heard me. You seem like a nice enough guy. Not a stalker or anything or a serial killer. So you can pick me up. Do you have a pen so you can write my address down?"

"Ah, yeah," Travis said.

"Great. I live at 61 LaFayette Street. It is in the Wellington Down's subdivision."

"Okay, 61 LaFayette Street in the Wellington Down's subdivision," Travis repeated.

"So I'll see you at six Friday night?"

"Yep. I'll pick you up at six," Travis said.

"Bye," Jade said.

"Bye." Travis hung the phone up as he thought about his dilemma. All of a sudden he was going to have to figure out a way to pick Jade up. She would be expecting him to pick her up in his candy apple–red BMW. He thought about using the excuse of the car being in the shop. The he wondered how much it would be to rent a candy apple–red BMW, but figured Enterprise Rent-A-Car or Alamo wouldn't just happen to have one sitting on their lots waiting to be rented. Somehow he was going to have to figure something out.

That Friday evening Travis rang the doorbell on the front door to Jade's home. It was a two-story brick home situated at the middle of a cul-de-sac. She came to the door wearing a tight-fitting off-white A-line dress that hugged her in all the right places. Again she looked as if she had just stepped out of the beauty salon.

She greeted Travis as she stepped out of the front door and locked it. "Hey, Wayne. I like a man who is punctual."

She hadn't invited him in or anything. He figured she wanted to make sure she made it to the dinner party early. He let her walk in front of him down the sidewalk and to the driveway.

"So this is your BMW?" Jade asked as she walked around to the passenger side door.

"Yep," Travis said, hoping she wouldn't hear the nervousness in his voice.

He opened the door for Jade to let her in and then returned to his side of the car to let himself in. Just after cranking the car he paused for a moment and said a very quick silent prayer to himself, praying he wouldn't get a scratch on Brent's car.

"Are you okay?" Jade asked.

Travis opened his eyes, clinched the wheel, and said, "Yeah, I'm good." Then he gingerly backed out of Jade's driveway.

It wasn't until he was fully out of her driveway and driving safely down her street that he spoke again. "You look very nice," he said.

"Thank you. You look pretty nice yourself," Jade said.

"Thanks," Travis said. Again Travis had returned to Brent's closet to put on the tuxedo he'd seen. It fit perfectly and now he actually looked like Richard Gere from the *Pretty Woman* movie.

They rode most of the way in silence as Travis paid as much attention as he could to the road and the other drivers. He would be glad when he got back home and could park the BMW back in the garage. Not only was he scared of damaging the car, but the trip to Jade's had already cost Travis twenty-five dollars in gas money. As soon as he'd cranked Brent's car he realized it was almost out of gas. He'd gone to the gas station to fill it up. But he realized that the gas meter was reading almost twenty dollars and it had only filled about five gallons worth of gas. So instead of filling up the tank, he decided to only pump twenty-five dollars worth.

"So, how was your day?" Jade asked.

"Good," Travis said. He didn't offer anything further. His mind was on figuring out where there would be a safe place to park downtown. The last thing he needed was to have Brent's car stolen.

Jade made a couple more attempts to make small talk with him and Travis answered the couple of closed-ended questions she had, but didn't offer any questions in reply to her. He knew he was acting a bit strange, but at that point he didn't care.

When they got downtown much of the parking close
to the restaurant was taken, so Travis ended up parking in a parking garage that cost him ten dollars. He
wasn't pleased with this additional expense, but did at
least feel slightly better about the safety of the car. So
far he had spent thirty-five dollars on his date out with
Jade. And by his calculations the savings he'd started
was now going to be down to about only forty-five dollars. He knew he was going to have to start watching
his spending and he was going to have to do better in
the savings department.

He still had a paycheck coming to him from the car
wash, and would have received a check from Alley's,
but was informed that his check would be used to buy
another alligator suit and to pay for the cleaning bill of
the customer whose clothing had been stained with red
ICEE juice.

As he tried to enjoy the night with Jade at the dinner
party it reminded him of something. And after racking
his brain, it came to him. In a way, Jade reminded him
of Gabrielle Union when she played the role of Eva in
the movie *Deliver Us from Eva*. In the movie Gabrielle
was a beautiful business woman who focused on work
and had a heart of ice. Jade seemed like she was on
some sort of mission that night and the mission wasn't
really to get to know Travis better.

Travis felt more like an arm piece or an accessory to
Jade. Her demeanor toward him changed drastically
when they hit the doors of the restaurant and Jade saw
some of her coworkers. She clutched on to Travis as if
the two had been a couple and had known one another
for years. She was trying to put up some kind of front
for them. It was a fakeness that Travis had never noticed before and he didn't like it at all. He played along

with her game of "this is my boyfriend" as he enjoyed the ambiance and food.

At the end of the night he delivered her back home. At her home she thanked him for accompanying her to the dinner party and failed to invite him in her house when he walked her to the front door. There she gave him a peck on the cheek and said good-bye.

Upon pulling the BMW back into the garage, Travis breathed a sigh of relief. He was never going to do that again. Borrowing a few pieces of clothing was one thing, but taking his friend's expensive sports car was a whole different story. And again he'd dished out way more money than he'd had to dish out and needed to spend. If he kept on putting up the false pretense of being Wayne, he was going to be broke again, real soon.

Chapter 14

The next Sunday morning, Travis kept his vow and arose bright and early to make it back to New Hope Church to attend the 8:00 service. This time he cooked himself a breakfast of scrambled eggs, grits, and country ham. The meal didn't taste like his mother's, but it would do. Once he finished eating his stomach was full and satisfied.

Just before leaving he grabbed his Bible, a pen, and his notebook. He also grabbed the woman's Bible he'd picked up a few Sundays before with hopes that he would see her again and would be able to return it to her. If he remembered right her name was Marla.

The regular pastor had returned from his vacation so he preached that morning instead of Phillip. Travis still hoped he would get the opportunity to talk to Phillip and Shelby after one of the services to at least say hi to them. In retrospect, he now wished he had exchanged numbers with the couple at the end of the marriage retreat, but he had let Beryl handle the matter of getting contact information for them.

Travis sat through and enjoyed the first service, then stayed for the second service. As he had done a few Sundays before, he moved up closer to the front of the church and placed his notebook and the Bibles in the seat next to him, saving the seat just in case he saw the woman.

A few minutes later he saw the woman walk down the aisle, also toward the front as she looked for a seat. He made eye contact. She smiled and joined him.

"Good morning, Marla," Travis said.

"Good morning," the woman replied.

Travis moved the books from the seat so she could sit down; then he handed her her Bible. "Here you are."

"Thank you. I've been looking all over for this. I thought I might have left it here but couldn't remember."

"You're welcome. You got out of here so fast that Sunday that I couldn't find you to give it back, so I just figured that maybe I would get the pleasure of seeing you again and would be able to return it to you."

As she had done a few Sundays ago, she blushed. "Thank you." Marla's voice was soft-spoken and had a wholesome quality to it that Travis liked. She was also shorter than him even with her high heels on. Her hair was short with full-bodied tight curls and she reminded Travis a great deal of his older sister.

"I had to go over to the nursing home to see my great aunt. She looks forward to my Sunday visits."

"That is sweet. How old is your aunt?" Travis asked.

"She's ninety-six," Marla said.

"Wow, I hope we can all make it to that age," Travis said.

"Me too. She is completely in her right mind, and if her legs and hips would work a little better for her, she'd still be at home taking care of herself."

"That is so nice that you go and visit her at the nursing home."

"Yeah, she likes my company, but she also likes sweets. I had to go to the store to pick up a few of her favorite candies before heading over to the home," Marla said.

The worship and praise music for the second service began playing. People started standing up and clapping their hands.

"I am so very sorry," Marla said. "Please tell me your name again."

"Travis."

"I'm sorry. I thought that was it but just wanted to make sure."

They both stood and joined the congregation in clapping their hands and singing with the musicians and the choir. When the pastor preached his sermon on accountability, Travis did just as he had the first Sunday he had attended. He jotted down scriptures and notes, while mouthing out many of them as he wrote and the pastor spoke. The message from the second service was almost a carbon copy of the first service.

Again Travis could see that Marla was impressed with what she thought was the spiritual gift of knowledge that he had. And to Travis it felt nice to have someone admire him for a change. At the end of service Travis walked with Marla to the foyer of the church.

With both services being over, it was time for them to part ways, although Travis wished he didn't have to. He enjoyed talking to Marla.

"Well, I guess I'll see you next Sunday," Travis said.

"Oh, okay. Are you not going to the fellowship hall?" Marla asked.

"To the fellowship hall? For what?"

"Dinner. They have plates in there."

"Oh, I didn't know. Sure."

They walked to the fellowship hall, and each got a plate. They found two seats at a table and ate together and talked. Travis was pleased to have been able to spend more time with Marla and to also get a meal on top of everything else.

***

Throughout the next couple of weeks Travis ended up getting a job with a cab company. He figured that with driving a cab he'd be able to make money and would also be able to get around without having to wait for the bus. But his stint there was short-lived. He had been given the graveyard shift to drive, and on his third night working, one of his new coworkers had been robbed at gunpoint.

Travis realized that he didn't want to put himself in a situation like that and turned his keys back in to his new boss. He had also found that it wasn't easy to just take the cab anywhere he wanted to go, which defeated one of his original purposes for wanting to drive the cab in the first place.

It had been over three weeks since he'd seen Beryl and the boys. And he still had not made contact with her. At first he called her hoping she would answer the phone so he could talk with her. Then he finally decided to go ahead and leave her a few quick cryptic messages—messages that wouldn't hint that he knew anything about her new friend and job loss.

But he still hadn't heard from her. He was starting to get a bit worried and had even contemplated calling one of her family members but knew that his calls and questions would fall on deaf ears. Her family didn't have too much to do with him ever since they had separated and finally divorced.

He was sure that her family had probably gotten an earful the last couple of months that he hadn't had contact with her. They wouldn't be forthcoming with any information about their loved one.

He'd gone out on a few more fun dates with Tory and had also gone out on a date with Jade, taking her to a touring play. Travis had enjoyed the comedy throughout the play; Jade, on the other hand, acted as if she was bored and had somewhere else to be. Travis didn't know why he was trying so hard to impress a woman who obviously wasn't that in to him. But every time he looked at her body, he figured that had something to do with it.

He figured that at the rate they were going, he'd never get a chance to spend any real quality time with her. He'd told himself that after that night he was going to let Jade go on her merry little way. He hoped she'd find whatever she was looking for because he'd come to the realization that whatever she was looking for obviously wasn't him.

In keeping with his vow to attend church more, he had attended back-to-back services each Sunday. And he and Marla attended the second service together. He had even started leaving the first service to stand in the foyer to greet her so that they could find a seat together.

Travis was starting to find that much of what he was being taught in service he was retaining. He had even found himself reading through the Bible at home. What he found was that he was finding what he was learning by rote interesting. He was especially interested in the series the pastor was preaching on accountability.

The sermons on accountability were touching him deeply. He was learning that there was not only a worldly accountability, but a spiritual accountability as well. One couldn't be accountable in one area and not be accountable in another area. Through the teachings he was able to see and understand ways in which he wasn't being accountable when it came to his life and especially when it came to his family and taking care of his boys. He also realized he hadn't been accountable during his marriage to his wife.

Each Sunday he'd hoped to get a chance to see and talk with Phillip, but was unable to because of the number of people vying for the man's attention after each service. Travis had started to think that he was going to have to see about just contacting him thorough the church to say hello.

Travis had just about given up hope of talking to Phillip, but one Sunday, Travis ended up running into Phillip and two other gentlemen as he came from the bathroom. Phillip immediately recognized him.

"Travis?" Phillip said.

"Hey, Phillip," Travis greeted him.

Travis extended his hand for Phillip to shake in greeting. But Phillip gave him a hug instead. "It's good to see you. What in the world? What are you doing here in Silvermont?" Phillip asked.

"Well, I've been here for the past few months, and started coming to New Hope a couple of months ago. I came that Sunday you preached."

"Oh really? You should have told me you were here," Phillip said.

"I did try a couple of times, but you run with an entourage the size of the president's."

Phillip looked at the two guys who were accompanying him and smiled. "Not that big."

Travis was just glad to finally be able to talk to him. "So I see you preach sometimes too."

"Yeah, normally I work with the youth ministry, mainly the teens," Phillip said. Then he went on to say, "So how are you all doing? How are Beryl and your boys?" Phillip looked around as if looking for Travis's family.

Travis hung his head for a brief second and took a breath before saying, "Beryl and I are no longer together." He waited for Phillip to rub in an "I told you so."

Phillip placed his hand on Travis's shoulder. "Man, I am sorry to hear that. I really am."

Then, as he had done so many times at the marriage retreat, Phillip paused to allow Travis to talk. He stood there ready to listen.

Travis trusted Phillip and knew he could confide in him. "Phillip, I should have listened to you. You tried to talk to me at the retreat, and all I could think about was going back to bed and getting some more sleep." He took another deep breath.

"I should have been paying attention to what Beryl was trying to tell me all along. I was all talk and no show. When she needed me to be a man of my word I wasn't. When we got back she showed me that she wasn't playing. That retreat was my last chance and I blew it." Travis paused again as he thought about the fact that it looked like Beryl was swiftly moving on with her life and all he seemed to be doing was playing games with women, while not having a pot to cook in or a window to throw the leftovers out of.

As if knowing just what Travis needed to hear, Phillip said, "Travis, don't be so hard on yourself. We all have lessons to learn, and sometimes we learn lessons the easy way and other times we learn them the hard way."

Travis nodded, fully understanding what Phillip meant.

"What I've learned in life is that we have to pay attention to the lessons we have learned so we don't make the same or similar mistakes over and over again. Then we also have to look at any good that may have come from what we deem as a loss in our lives," Phillip said.

"I can assure you I don't want anything like this to happen again. If I am ever blessed to be able to find another woman, then I will not make these same mistakes again." Travis shook his head. "But I can't for the life of me see any good that has come from all of this. I am still struggling with that part."

One of the guys with Phillip tapped him on his shoulder. "Okay," Phillip said to the guy.

Travis understood this to mean that Phillip needed to get going wherever he was already headed to when Travis saw him.

"Travis, I encourage you to pray about your current situation and the Lord will lead you in the direction you should go in. Just trust in Him. He will not lead you astray."

"Thank you, Phillip. I really appreciate what you've told me, and this time I will take heed."

Phillip pulled a card out of his pocket and handed it to Travis. "Call me."

Travis looked at the card. It was Phillip's business card. He was the owner of a local car dealership. The card had his office number and cell phone number.

"Give me a call sometime," Phillip reiterated.

"I will," Travis said.

"And welcome to Silvermont. I'll talk with you later," Phillip said.

"Thank you," Travis said.

He returned to the church service and tried to concentrate on what the pastor was saying. The sermon was one that continued the pastor's series about accountability. The pastor preached that accountability starts from within. And that the Lord holds His people accountable for the time they spend, the money they are blessed with, the gifting God has given them, the knowledge they posses, as well as each person's mental intentions.

Travis knew he fell short in each of these areas. He squandered his time, money, and his intentions. Even though Marla thought he had a gift of knowledge he himself did not think so. He had no idea what his gifting might be, but did feel pretty sure that if he did know what his gifting was, he would probably be squandering it also.

It didn't help matters either that, throughout the sermon, Travis's thoughts kept veering toward his earlier conversation with Phillip. He continued to ponder on what kind of positive things could be extracted from the situation he was currently in. And he was coming to the full realization that he could not blame anyone else for his actions. No one else made him do any of the things he did. He was in control of his actions, he was the one who chose for himself, he'd made some very wrong choices.

He alone was the one who got himself into his current situation and he was going to have to get himself out of his situation, plain and simple. He was going to have to make some changes in his life. He wanted to be accountable.

Chapter 15

If Travis had looked at a calendar that Friday morning, he might have been a little bit forewarned—that is, if he were a superstitious person. Travis knew it was Friday, but hadn't realized it was August 13th. What Travis did know was that it was payday. He'd been working at a job for the county as a maintenance technician for a month now. He got paid every two weeks. He had been delighted to get his check and go to the bank and cash it that evening.

When he checked his PO Box he found a letter in the mail from the child support office stating that they were going to start garnishing his pay for back child support. According to the letter, they were going to take $200 per pay period out of his check. Travis couldn't believe what he was reading.

It seemed as if Beryl must have filed for child support behind his back. First she wouldn't answer his calls and now she was going through the system to get money from him. He wondered if she had completely lost her mind. Then he thought about it, and tried not to let his temper get the best of him.

He was the one who avoided her phone calls. He was the one who hadn't sent her a dime in months. So he wasn't completely innocent. So how could he really blame Beryl? It wasn't like his boys could live on air, but he really wished it wouldn't be up to the system to make him care for his children.

At the same time it baffled him that for months Beryl called him sometimes on a daily basis, and now he had not heard a thing from her in over a month. He started to get a little worried, but remembered how she was acting the last time he saw her. The last thing on her mind was him. She was all into Urkel.

When he got home that evening from work, he still was not pleased with the child support notification he received. He was even less happy with the note that was posted on the front door of the house. It was a letter from the homeowner's association. The letter said that he had forty-eight hours to cut his grass or he would be fined.

He'd been trying to cut the grass every other week, but had put it off for the last month. Looking at the grass he had to admit that it was long overdue to be cut. He was in no mood to cut it right then, but from the looks of it, now that he had waited so long to cut it, it was going to take him twice as much time as it normally would have.

After putting his wallet away and changing his clothing, he trudged back outside to the shed to pull out the lawn mower, and started cutting the grass. He had just cut the first strip of grass on the front lawn when he turned around to cut another strip. When he looked up at the sky his eyes widened. There was a dark cloud coming up and it looked as if the bottom of the sky was going to fall out at any moment.

Picking his speed up he was able to mow the width of the lawn with two more trips back and forth, but that had been it. First a fat drop hit his nose and spattered into his eyes. Then other fat drops fell in rapid succession. A bolt of lightning lit up the sky; then he heard a loud thunder clap.

Travis quickly made his way back to the shed to put the mower away By the time he closed the door to the shed and got back into the house, he was cold and soaked. He took his wet clothing off. Even though the lightning persisted with the thunder close behind, he took a chance taking a quick warm shower.

Once he was out of the shower and dried off, he felt a little better; that is, until he looked at his cell phone and saw that he had two messages. One was from a number he did not recognize and the other from Beryl. His heart started to race.

He quickly punched in his code to retrieve his messages. He checked the first message from Beryl in which she asked for him to call. Unlike so many of the other messages she'd left in the past, she sounded nonchalant, almost as if she really didn't care whether he called back. Travis didn't know what to think. He didn't know if she was mad or if she had really just given up on him all together. In the back of his mind he wondered if she was really just calling to gloat because she was finally going to get child support out of him.

The second message was from Brent. Subconsciously Travis looked around as if Brent could see through the phone lines how he'd been taking care of the house and his belongings. Brent said he hoped he was well, and that things were going well where he was. He also let Travis know that he'd be home on schedule: the first weekend in December.

Travis listened to Brent's message twice. He couldn't believe his ears. Brent had already been gone for three months and Travis hadn't managed to save more than $400. Where had the time gone? What had he been doing with his money? How had he really been spending his time? He thought about what the pastor had been teaching about accountability. He was unaccountable.

When checking the time that Beryl had left the message, Travis saw that she had left it less than an hour before. If he called her right now then maybe he'd actually get her. Before he dialed the number for her cell phone, Travis recalled the scripture James 1:19.

Wherefore, my beloved brethren, let every man be swift to hear, slow to speak, slow to wrath.

He took a deep breath just before dialing her number from memory. On the third ring Travis finally heard Beryl pick up on the other end.

"Hello," Beryl said.

"Hi," Travis said.

"Travis," Beryl said.

Travis thought her tone was surprisingly cordial.

"Yeah, how's it going?" Travis asked.

"Good, how about with you?" Beryl asked

"Things are okay."

"Well that's good," Beryl said.

"And the boys, how are they?" Travis asked.

"They are fine. Cameron is asleep already and Jayden is fighting sleep," Beryl said.

Travis smiled. Jayden always fought going to sleep ever since he was a baby. "He's still doing that, huh?"

"Yep," Beryl said.

Then there was a long pause between the two of them. Finally Beryl broke the silence. "So what's up, Travis?"

"What do you mean?"

"What I mean is, what is up? You called and left me a message yesterday. I am calling you back to see what you wanted."

Travis pulled the phone away from his ear and looked at it. "Yeah, I called you yesterday, and the day before that, and the week before that. I've been calling you for over a month now and you haven't seen fit to return any of those calls."

"Oh really? I don't recall any other calls. What I do recall is trying to call you multiple times without getting any calls returned to me," Beryl said.

"So is this tit for tat?" Travis asked.

"What do you mean by that?" Beryl asked.

"Just what I said. First I don't call you back so now you are just returning the favor?" Travis asked.

"Look, Travis, I don't want to argue. You called and left a message, and I called you back. Plain and simple. So, what's up?"

Travis was about to speak, then thought about the part of the scripture that said "slow to speak."

"Travis, are you still there?" Beryl asked.

"Yeah, I'm here."

"Did you get the letter about the child support?" Beryl asked.

"Yeah, I got it."

"Is that why you were calling?"

"No, that is not why I was calling. I got the letter today. I've been leaving messages for you well before I got the letter."

"I know you are probably not happy about getting it but I had no other choice," Beryl said.

"So, what has been going on with you? What happened to your job? I called there and some woman said you don't work there anymore."

"Are you asking to be nosey or do you really even care?"

"I care, Beryl."

"Well you could have fooled me," Beryl said. She let out a huff. "I was fired, over a trivial chain of events that I still can't believe happened."

"You were fired?" Travis asked in sheer disbelief.

"Yeah, some things happened. Some numbers were wrong in a couple of reports and I got one too many complaints from a couple of customers and the company decided to let me go," Beryl said.

"Wow, Beryl, I can't believe that," Travis said. "I am really sorry to hear that."

"I still can't believe it myself. But that seems like an eternity ago, and even though it still burns me up, I am getting over it."

"So are you and the boys okay?" Travis asked.

"We're fine."

"Now I understand why you need the child support so much," Travis said. "I am sorry it had to come to the point that you had to file for child support, but I fully understand."

"Umm humph," Beryl said. "Hold on a second, Travis."

Travis heard what sounded like Beryl placing her hand over the receiver of the phone to muffle what she was saying. Then it sounded like she'd taken her hand off the receiver and he clearly heard her chuckling on the other end.

"Sorry about that," Beryl said. "Now what were you saying?"

"I was just saying that I am sorry you lost your job and I understand that you need the money to help you and the boys get by," Travis said. He knew that $200 every other week would help Beryl a little, but not enough to really help make ends meet.

"Uh, yeah. Something like that," Beryl said.

Travis got the distinct feeling that Beryl wasn't too pressed about the amount of child support. Nor was she too pressed about much of anything.

"So you said Jayden is still up?"

He heard Beryl whisper the question, "Is Jayden still up?"

Then he heard a male voice in the background say, "No."

"Who was that?" Travis asked Beryl.

"That is my fiancé, Darrin," Beryl said.

"Say what? Your what?" Travis asked.

"My fiancé," Beryl repeated.

"Fiancé since when?" Travis asked.

"Since last week when he proposed to me in the Bahamas," Beryl said.

Travis took a step back and almost dropped the phone. He couldn't be hearing right.

"Look, Travis, I need to get off the phone. The boys are fine. Maybe you can call back and talk to them another time," Beryl said.

Travis was at a loss for words. He couldn't speak.

"Travis?" Beryl said. "Are you still there?"

"Ah, yeah, I'm here. Sure, I guess I'll talk to them soon." With the way Beryl was sounding he didn't know what to think.

"Talk with you later," Beryl said.

"Ah, yeah, bye," Travis said and clicked the phone off.

He stood in awe for a while trying to comprehend what he'd just heard. His ex-wife had found someone else and she was about to get married. The guy he had seen her with at Alley's was probably the Darrin guy she was talking about.

They hadn't been divorced a good year yet and Beryl was gallivanting out of the country with some other man. And she was allowing this other man fully into his son's lives. That man knew if his sons were asleep. That man had played with Travis's sons more recently than he had. That man was trying to take and succeeding in taking his place.

There was something about the Darrin guy he didn't like, and now he had even more of a reason not to like the man. He wanted to call Beryl back and tell her so, but knew he couldn't because then she'd know it was him in the Alley the Alligator suit.

Travis stepped over to the window of the bonus room and looked down at the rain-soaked lawn. The rain continued to pour down. He shook his head and whispered to himself, "When it rains it surely does pour."

Chapter 16

During the next week, Travis tried his best to pass the time without thinking about Beryl. He went out with Tory a couple of times, taking her to the movies again and to play miniature golf, but the twenty-something could not get his feelings out of the clouds. She was nice enough, but Travis was growing wearily tired of always being on the go with the girl. She always had to be doing something and there were times when Travis just wanted to sit still for a little while.

Not only did Tory always seem to literally want to play games, she didn't have any real direction. She was a hard worker, working her eight-to-five job all day, but she also liked to party hard. She rarely watched the news or talked about reading anything of substance, nor did she like to think or talk about the future. She was happy just living for the day.

In addition to her smoking habit turning Travis off, he had found that Tory didn't like children and she had no intention of having any children. This was a big problem for Travis because of his two little boys. He couldn't seriously date a woman who didn't get along with his two boys.

Then there was Jade. Travis had to do some real soul-searching there. Jade was older and sophisticated. She also seemed to have it all going on with her expensive clothing, expensive car, and the overall expensive taste to go with it all. But with all that expense and sophistication, Jade didn't seem to have any soul. And Travis got the distinct feeling that Jade was indeed a gold digger. It didn't seem to matter what Travis tried to do for her, it seemed to never be enough for her. In his book, money was important, but it wasn't everything.

One other thing that bothered him about Jade was that he really didn't know that much about her. He only knew some very basic and superficial things. He had no idea if she had any siblings, if she was originally from Silvermont, where she went to college, or what her favorite color was. And he couldn't see Jade around the boys, either. He didn't know if she had any motherly aspirations or what kind of feelings she had toward children.

Being a player was turning out harder than he had ever imagined. He was going to have to let his role as T.J. with Tory and his role of being Wayne with Jade go. There was no reason to continue wasting time with two women he knew weren't going to amount to anything long term for him.

Now when it came to his thoughts of Marla, they were warmer. She was a nice woman with wholesome qualities. He knew a little bit more about her. And now with his decision to drop Tory and Jade, he could spend his efforts getting to know Marla even better. That is, if he could focus long enough on Marla and stop stewing over the fact that Beryl had found another man to marry so quickly after their divorce.

"Here you are, sir and miss. Please have a seat right here and your waitress will be with you in just a moment," the hostess seating them said.

Travis pulled out Marla's chair so she could sit. Then he sat in the chair directly across from her.

"Thank you, Travis, for bringing me here," Marla said.

"Are you surprised?" Travis asked.

"I am. I can't believe you remembered my birthday. And that you remembered that Mama Lula's is my favorite restaurant."

"I've got a pretty good memory, I am told," Travis said.

"I mean I think I told you about my birthday and the restaurant that first day we ate dinner in the fellowship hall. It was just a friendly talk over dinner after church, nothing to write home about," Marla said.

"Nothing to write home about for someone who isn't interested," Travis said, making sure to make his interest known.

The waitress came to their table. "Hi, my name is Jody. How are y'all doing on this fine Sunday afternoon?"

"We're good, Jody. How about you?" Travis asked.

"I am just great. What can I get for you all to drink while you decide on what you would like to eat?"

Travis looked at Marla.

"I'll have a sweet tea," Marla said.

"Me too; I think I'll have a sweet tea as well," Travis said.

"Okay, let me go get your drinks. I'll be back in just a moment," Jody said.

When she left Marla said, "And thank you for taking me by the nursing home before coming out to eat."

"No problem. I know you like to visit your aunt on Sundays. I didn't want to come between you and your aunt. Besides, I didn't want your aunt to dislike me before she even met me," Travis said.

Marla chuckled.

Travis had rented a car to take Marla to the nursing home and out to dinner for her birthday. At first he was going to just get her a gift certificate for the mall, but after he won $200 on a scratch-off ticket he decided taking her out to dinner would be more personal and appropriate, especially since he was in the mode of trying to get to know her better.

The waitress returned with their iced teas and took their orders. While they waited for their food, Travis learned that Marla was originally from Houma, Louisiana. And it just so happened that she had moved to North Carolina for a change a month before Hurricane Katrina hit the Gulf Coast. She felt fortunate to have been able to move with all of her belongings before devastation hit the area she formerly lived in.

While eating dinner Travis learned more about Marla. He learned that she had a teenage son who was in college in South Carolina, and that her mother and father were still living in Louisiana. She loved family and called them at least once a week and her goal was to return to visit them at least once a year. Thus far she had been able to do so.

It was clear that she had caring genes, loving genes, and motherly genes. She cared not only about family but she also cared about her friends. Travis liked to talk, but Marla liked to talk even more. Information about her life spilled out as she talked.

Here and there he would interject information about himself. He told her about his mother and sisters and the fact that he never knew who his father was. But he never bought up Beryl's name and didn't tell her that he had two little boys. He feared that if he brought their names up then Marla would want to start talking about them more. She would want to know more information about his relationship with his ex-wife now and his sons.

Over the next couple of weeks, while he found it very refreshing to talk with Marla, he felt bad about deceiving her about his spiritual status. He never lied to her about why he seemed to know so much about the scripture and the Word during the church services, he just hadn't divulged the truth to her. He'd never let on that he had been cheating by going to the first service to be clairvoyant about what the pastor was preaching about.

As he got to know Marla better and better, he felt as if he could feel the little angel and devil sitting on each one of his shoulders. The angel nagged him to come clean with her and tell her the truth about himself, while the devil poked him with encouragement to be a playa and play on.

If Travis could have had a crystal ball he would have come clean with Marla that day at Mama Lula's. The crystal ball would have warned him of events to come. He would have taken the opportunity to tell her all about himself. He'd tell her about his ex-wife, his two little boys, and about his being a double agent at church.

Chapter 17

Going out to dinner after church had become a ritual for Travis and Marla. It was Labor Day weekend and they were sitting at a booth in the window of the Piccadilly Cafeteria in the mall. Marla and Travis had enjoyed the second service together, and now they were eating the desserts they had chosen.

Marla was telling Travis about an incident at her job. He wasn't going to be able to tell her anything about his job in turn because he had been let go from the county when they downsized. He was one of the last hired and ended up being one of the first fired.

Travis heard someone knocking on the glass of the window where they were sitting. On the other side of the window Travis saw his oldest son, Cameron, knocking, and his baby boy, Jayden, with his face mashed against the glass.

Cameron smiled and waved when he saw that he'd finally gotten his dad's attention. Jayden, too, pulled his face back and waved at his dad. When Travis looked up he saw Beryl holding hands with her Urkel-looking fiancé. He dropped the forkful of cheesecake he was about to put into his mouth and made contact with Beryl and her new man.

Seeing the exchange between Travis and the people outside of the window, Marla asked, "Who are they?" Her smile was unassuming.

"Those are my sons," Travis said almost under his breath.

He wiped his hands with his napkin and stood to walk out of the restaurant to greet his boys and finally confront the man who was doing his best to take his place.

Before Travis could take a step, Marla said, "They are your what?" He could hear the understandable confusion in her voice.

He smiled and waved back at his little boys. He couldn't focus on Marla's confusion right then. He had to get outside. "I'll be right back," he said to her.

His feet couldn't move fast enough. The people who were standing in line to pay for their food were like human obstacles for him. He pushed past them, barely uttering an excuse me.

"Sir, sir," he heard the cashier say.

"I'm not leaving. My friend is still sitting in there with the check. I'll be right back." Then he kept walking.

As soon as his boys saw him come around the corner, they ran up to Travis. He picked them both up, each in an arm. The boys hugged him just as if they had missed him the entire time they had been apart. They hugged him tightly as if they didn't want to let go. The smile on his sons' faces held genuine smiles, different from the ones he'd seen on their faces when Beryl's fiancé played with them. Those laughs and smiles had been more like "I just want to have fun with someone" smiles. These smiles were "I love you, Daddy" smiles. And it warmed Travis's heart to the core.

"Hello, Travis," Beryl said. Her voice was cool.

"Beryl," Travis responded to the greeting.

"Hi, Daddy," Cameron said.

"Hey, Daddy," Jayden said.

"Hey, boys." Travis smiled into the eyes of both of the boys.

"Where have you been, Daddy?" Cameron asked.

"Daddy's been trying to take care of some things," Travis said. It was all he could offer at the time to his son.

"I missed you, Daddy," Cameron said.

"Daddy has missed you two boys too," Travis said. Tears threatened to fill his eyes. How could he have stayed away from his two little men for so long?

Jayden squirmed down out of his father's arm and ran back over to his mother. Beryl picked the boy up, and when she did, Travis saw the rock that was on Beryl's left ring finger. The thing seemed to glisten in the light that was beaming from outside. It would make the engagement ring he'd given her years ago look diminutive if the two were placed side by side.

"Hello, I am Darrin. You must be Travis." Darrin extended his hand to shake Travis's. His voice was deeper than he had remembered it being from the day they'd had the altercation at Alley's. For some reason Travis really expected it to sound more high-pitched.

"I am," Travis said. He stuck his hand out with reluctance and shook Darrin's hand.

Darrin's handshake was feeble to Travis. Travis liked people who had a firm handshake. Travis returned the handshake with a firm one. He held the shake for a second longer than need be, wanting to continue shaking and squeezing until he broke a couple of bones in the guy's hand. But he'd gone ahead and let go, glaring at him. There was something that Travis did not like about the guy at all.

"So, Travis, what are you doing here in Silvermont?" Beryl asked. She looked over at the woman sitting in the restaurant and gave her a polite smile.

"What am I doing in Silvermont?" Travis asked. "What are you all doing here?"

"I live here now," Beryl said.

"Say what?" Travis said. "When did you move here?"

"We've been here about a month now," Beryl said. "And what about you?" Again Beryl glanced over at the woman sitting in the restaurant. It was obvious that she was curious who he was having dinner with.

"I live here as well," Travis said.

"Oh, really. So this is where you moved to," Beryl said. "I knew you had moved somewhere in this county, but didn't know you had actually moved to Silvermont. What a small world."

"It is a small world indeed," Travis said.

"Daddy, Daddy, can we come with you?" Cameron asked.

Travis looked toward Beryl and Darrin, then back to his son. He knew that it wasn't feasible for him to take either of the boys with him today. He needed some time to sit and talk with Beryl about setting up some time to be with the boys, plus he had caught a ride with Marla that afternoon.

"Not today, son. I am going to talk with your mom some more to see about setting up some time for you to visit, especially now that I know how close you all are to me now," Travis said.

Cameron whined at the answer he received. Jayden laid his head down on his mother's shoulder. Out of the corner of his eye, he saw Darrin take a long glance at Beryl, as he let out a sigh as if he was bored.

Travis didn't know completely why, but this gesture by Darrin really started to make him almost lose his cool. The only thing that helped him keep his emotions at bay was the fact that his little boys were standing right there. He didn't want the boys' smiles to turn into tears as they had the day at Alley's.

As far as Travis was concerned Darrin could just go somewhere and disappear. He wanted to talk to Beryl alone and couldn't talk with her like he wanted to with Darrin looming around. The guy acted like Travis was beneath him. He acted as if Travis were nothing and he too just wished Travis would disappear off the face of the earth.

"Beryl, I would like to see about setting up some time to spend with the boys," Travis said.

"We can work that out I am sure," Beryl said.

Darrin looked at his watch. Travis couldn't resist not keeping his mouth shut. "I'm sorry, am I keeping you all from doing something?"

"Yeah," Beryl said. "We just got out of church and had to run by here to pick up something. We haven't eaten yet. We're headed back home to eat."

Travis knew what that meant. Beryl had cooked a full Sunday dinner, like she used to do when they were married. He could just imagine that she had cooked a roast, and mashed potatoes with gravy. She had probably made some turnip greens and homemade lemonade. And if he really knew his ex-wife, he was sure that she had made a chocolate cake for dessert.

For the first time he noticed that the four were all dressed up in Sunday attire. They looked like the average happy little family strolling around the mall after church. The only problem was that they weren't actually a family.

"Besides, aren't you being rude to your dinner guest in there?" Beryl asked.

Travis had almost forgotten about Marla. He looked over at her and saw that she didn't look too happy, as she had already balled up her napkin and put it on the plate atop her unfinished apple pie. He could tell Marla wasn't pleased as she sat there with her arms crossed and she stared in thought down at their empty dinner plates.

"Yeah. Beryl, I'll give you a call to see when we can set something up so I can see the boys," Travis said.

"Okay," Beryl said.

Travis gave his oldest son a kiss on his forehead and then put him down. "Daddy is going to call your mom and we'll talk so that you and Jayden can spend some time with me."

"Okay, Daddy," Cameron said. He walked over to his mother, leaned on her, and put his arm around her waist.

"Nice to meet you, man," Darrin said.

Travis wasn't about to say "same here." So he just gave Darrin a single nod.

Then the mock family of four walked out of the front doors of the mall. Travis watched them until they were out of sight. Once he couldn't see them anymore, he returned inside the restaurant and joined Marla at the table.

As soon as he sat back down in the booth, Marla started asking him questions.

"So, those were your sons, huh?" Her tone was that of hurt and shock.

"Yes," Travis replied.

"And was that your ex-wife?" Marla asked. When asking this question, Marla's tone didn't seem so hurt. He guessed because Beryl had acted with warmth toward the woman.

"Yes, that was my ex-wife," Travis said. "And with her was her new fiancé." This he said with sarcasm.

"Do they live around here?" Marla asked.

"Yes, they do," Travis said. He was still surprised by that revelation.

"They live right here in Silvermont and you've never even told me anything about them?" Marla asked. "What is up with that?"

"There is nothing up with that. I didn't know they lived in Silvermont until a few minutes ago," Travis tried to explain. "I don't know why I hadn't told you about them before now."

"I know why," Marla said. "It is because you didn't want me to know. Here I am spilling my guts to you about any and everything. But you don't really see me as someone worthy enough to share anything of real importance with obviously."

Travis reached for Marla's hands, but she pulled back.

"Look, Marla, it isn't like that, I assure you. It's just that . . ." His voice trailed off, not really knowing how to explain it all.

"See, just like I said. It is okay for me to tell you about me and my life, but you don't want to share your life with me."

"No, Marla. Honestly, it is a long story."

Marla clutched her purse under her arm and slid out of the booth. "Well, Travis, I don't have time for any long stories. You've had more than enough time to share any long stories with all the time you and I have been talking on the phone, coupled with all the times we've been out."

Travis slipped out of his side of the booth also. "Marla, look, I'm sorry. I really am. There is no excuse, I realize that."

"Well, keep those sorrys to yourself. I don't have time to hear them right now. Bye, Travis." Marla left the table and headed straight out of the door.

Travis sat back down in the seat and put his head in his hands. He had gotten himself in a mess with Marla. His ex-wife had found another man, his sons perhaps another father, and now he was back to square one in the relationship game of life.

Chapter 18

That night and for the next week and a half, Travis tried to no avail to reach Marla. His calls went directly to voice mail. He wondered if she was even checking the numerous messages he'd been leaving her. He had even sent her multiple texts of apology but failed to get any responses back. He didn't see her anywhere that next Sunday at church.

He felt really bad about the way he'd handled things with Marla. If he had just been himself, his true self, then he wouldn't be in the situation he was in. He should have told her that he was knowledgeable only because he'd been to the previous church service and knew firsthand what the pastor was going to preach about. He should have reciprocated information about himself when she was telling him about her life.

Why hadn't he come clean in the first place? Was it because he was trying to be some sort of player? Was it because he didn't think she would like him for who he really was? Or was it because deep down he didn't really care enough about the woman to tell her his innermost thoughts and feelings. Maybe she was right about that part.

And when he really thought more about it, Travis realized that Marla deserved more than what he had to offer her at the time. He needed to do some work on himself—there needed to be a major overhaul on his life. For years he had stressed over his outer appearance. He'd worried about his height compared to other men and how women would see him. He'd also worried about what people would think about his torn-up teeth before he finally got them fixed at the dentist. And in all that time, he had never really looked at himself on the inside. His heart needed an overhaul, his spirit needed an overhaul, and his finances truly needed a major overhaul. The goals he previously had in life needed to be seriously revamped.

As he sat in the quiet of the bonus room, he shook his head, wondering who in the world he was to think that he of all people could or even should be a player. He hadn't been able to handle one good and devoted wife; how was he supposed to handle multiple women? And what did he have to offer any woman? Shelter? No. Financial security? No. Being dependable? No. Being a true spiritual man of God? No. That checklist was seriously delinquent. If he had spent half as much of his time working hard to keep a steady job while he was married instead of working hard to find ways to be out of work, maybe his marriage would have survived.

Even though he was being hard on himself, Travis knew there had to be some good qualities about himself. He thought about it. He was a faithful man. Not once had he ever cheated on his wife, or seriously looked in the direction of another woman while he was married to Beryl. And in his heart he was still faithful to her. With all the dating he had done since he and Beryl separated and divorced, not once had he been with any other woman intimately. He wondered if Beryl could say the same. He didn't even want to think about how the Urkel-looking Darrin might have tried to seduce her down in the tropical islands.

There was definitely something he didn't like about that guy. He was cocky, and a little bit too self-assured for Travis's taste. And he didn't even seem like Beryl's type. Beryl's type was more like him. From the looks of Darrin's clothing and the rock of a ring he'd presented to Beryl, it looked as if Darrin didn't have any financial problems. But he figured Darrin's money was probably a very inviting enticement for Beryl.

As he remembered it, Beryl was always nagging him about money and the finances. But Travis had to stop that train of thought and lay shame to the devil. Beryl had not always been nagging him about money and finances. And when she did talk about the money she had been within her full rights. Travis had not been carrying his weight as a husband and father. He was often lazy and let her carry the load and burden of making sure their household stayed afloat. So how could he blame her for gravitating toward Darrin? Now she had a man by her side who looked as if he was taking care of that whole burden for her. And Beryl should never have had to go through the court to get Travis to pay for his own children. For this he was ashamed.

He shook his head again. What a mess he'd gotten himself into. Then he thought about the advice from his friend Phillip that day he'd seen him at church. He needed to look to the Lord and pray about it. The Lord would help lead him.

Travis kneeled down in front of the recliner he was sitting in and bowed his head into his hands to pray. He prayed his prayer, out loud saying, "Dear Lord, I come to you this day in prayer. Lord, I have made an awful mess. Lord, I understand now that I've made some mistakes. Okay, Lord, I have come to realize that I have made quite a few mistakes. And I want to make up for any mistakes that I have made. Lord, I want to be a better man. I want to be stronger in you, Lord; I want my finances to be stronger; I want to be the man

I am supposed to be to my children and that I should have been to Beryl. Lord, please forgive me for not being accountable.

"Lord, I know I can't do this on my own. So I am asking for your guidance and help. And, Lord, I pray that I did not hurt Marla too bad. Please help heal her heart. And, Lord, I know I shouldn't be asking for so much when I have done so little in my life to honor and please you, but, Lord, I just ask one last thing. Please protect my children and their mother. I know deep down in my heart I don't like the fact that Beryl is now with another man, but, Lord, my spirit keeps telling me that man is no good for her. So please keep her safe, Lord; take care of her.

"I thank you, Lord, in your son Jesus' name. Amen."

Travis got up off of his knees and felt as if a burden had been lifted from his shoulders. He had some things to focus on now. He was going to make some changes in his life starting right then. And he knew that he was not going to have to make all of the changes by himself. He had the Lord on his side.

Once he was finished praying, Travis realized two very important things. First, he thought about his previous self-checklist of the kinds of things he could offer any sane woman. He had to change those no's to yes's; and, secondly, he didn't want just *any* sane woman, he wanted Beryl. He wanted his ex-wife back.

Travis sat at the desk in his friend Brent's home office. It was there that he'd started looking at all of his finances. He started breaking down his current expenses and bills, and had also started a spreadsheet of sorts to list future bills he would need to pay once he was out on his own again.

The spreadsheet he had concocted was basically drawn by hand since he didn't have a computer to put one on. He listed his current expenses, like food, transportation for the bus and taxis he'd been taking, and his cell phone bill. Then he also put expenses like gas, water, rent, child support, electricity, and savings, as well as tithes and offering on his sheet.

Mentally he had to prepare for the future and he had to do the same physically. As soon as he started getting paid, he would start putting money away for the categories on the spreadsheet as if he currently had the expenses. That way he'd know what he could and or couldn't handle in the upcoming months.

With a little less than two months to go until Brent was to return, Travis knew he would have to step things up into high gear. After months of living at Brent's he had only managed to save $333. He needed a job, and not just any job. He needed a job that potentially had good pay, good benefits, and the potential for growth. But most of all he needed to be able to keep the job once he found it. Travis knew that was a tall order, but he had the Lord on his side so he commenced looking for that perfect job, knowing that faith without works would be dead.

Travis scoured the classified section of the newspaper looking for jobs. He had applied for several and had even had an interview for a call center position. He closed the folder with his spreadsheet.

He looked down at his cell phone, hoping that there was a message or missed call indication from Beryl, but there was nothing. It had been almost two weeks since he'd seen Beryl and the boys in the mall. He'd called and left her several messages but she hadn't called him back. He knew it was karma and payback all rolled up into one. Now he was the one calling and leaving messages only to have his calls ignored.

His cell phone rang.

"Hello," Travis answered.

"Hello. May I speak with Mr. Travis Highgate?" the person at the other end of the line said.

"This is he."

"Hi, Mr. Highgate. This is Melanie Shumaker in the HR department of the Escape Inns call center."

"Oh, yes. Hi, Ms. Shumaker," Travis said. He hoped she was calling with good news.

"Mr. Highgate, I am calling to see if you are still interested in the position for call center attendant for which you applied."

"I sure am," Travis said with hopeful expectation in his voice.

"Great. Well, we would like to offer the position to you."

"Thank you. I would like to accept," Travis said almost before the woman could finish offering him the position.

"Okay, well great then," Melanie Shumaker said. "Your hours would be from eight to five, Monday to Friday."

"Yes, I remember," Travis said.

"And I want you to know that there was a typing error on the pay that we are offering for the position you applied for," Ms. Shumaker said.

"Oh, really?" Travis asked, ready to hear that the pay was lower than he originally expected.

"Yes, the pay is actually two dollars more per hour."

"Really?"

"Yes, sorry about that. I hope this information will further solidify the answer to accept that you've already given me," Ms. Shumaker said.

"It most certainly does," Travis said. He felt like a child on Christmas morning receiving more gifts than he was anticipating.

"There will be two weeks of training. The first day will mainly be orientation," Ms. Shumaker said. "The orientation and training will be the same as your regular working hours from eight to five."

"Wonderful," Travis said.

"Okay, then, we'll see you bright and early at eight o'clock," Melanie said.

"Eight o'clock it is," Travis replied.

"You can report to the HR office first, and bring your social security card and ID with you. We'll have you fill out other pertinent paperwork when you get here," Ms. Shumaker said.

"Thank you, Ms. Shumaker. I look forward to meeting you and being an employee of Escape Inns," Travis said.

"Wonderful. I can see already that you will be an excellent call sales agent for the company. You are polite and very cordial," Ms. Shumaker said.

"Thank you and have a wonderful evening," Travis said.

"You too." And with that Ms. Melanie Shumaker hung up.

Travis jumped up from his seat and shouted, "Yes." The Lord had opened a door for him that gave him all that he'd asked for. He would be working at a great place, with great pay and benefits.

He went straight to his bedroom to look for an outfit to wear for his first day of work. He found two pairs of pants and a couple of dress shirts. There wasn't much for him to choose from in his own wardrobe that looked business-casual enough to wear, but if he had to, he would continue to wash his two pairs of pants

and change shirts often to make it look like he had
more clothing than he really had. He had contemplated
going to the Goodwill to find some shirts and pants before, and now he would seriously revisit that idea.

He ironed one of the pairs of pants and the light blue
dress shirt he owned. He laid out his socks, shoes, and
underwear so that they would be ready in the morning.
Then he headed down to the kitchen to pack a lunch.
He made two sandwiches and put some chips in a
sandwich zip bag. He found a thermos in Brent's cabinet and he filled it with grape juice. If he could help it,
he wasn't going to spend any extra money eating out or
at the vending machines.

That night Travis headed to bed early. He set two
alarms: the one on his nightstand and the one on his
cell phone. Although he wasn't the type to oversleep or
miss an alarm, he didn't want to chance it with this job.
He'd had enough problems and mishaps with jobs in
the past and he was determined for that not to be the
case with this job.

That next morning Travis awoke a few minutes before
either alarm went off. He took his shower, got dressed,
and made a breakfast of oatmeal, coffee, a slice of but-
tered and jelly toast, and a glass of orange juice. His
stomach was full and satisfied by the time he took his
seat on the city bus. As he rode toward his new job, he
wondered why the company was starting him out on a
Friday, but figured it might be easier to do orientation
on a Friday and full training of employees starting the
full week on a Monday.

He had arrived early at the HR office at 7:50 and was
sitting outside of it when the first HR person arrived.

"Hi. Can I help you?" the woman who was fumbling
with her keys to open her office said.

"Ah, yes, I am here for my first day at work. My name is Travis Highgate."

"Oh," the woman said. "Oh, my."

"Is there a problem?" Travis asked. "I spoke with a Melanie Shumaker and she said to be here at eight."

"Mr. Highgate. I am so very sorry." She turned and extended her hand to Travis. "I am Ms. Shumaker."

"Oh, hi, Ms. Shumaker," Travis said. He was just about to be very concerned by the woman's vagueness and actions, but she didn't seem like there was a huge problem, just something interesting or ironic.

"I really must apologize. Did I not tell you that the first day was this Monday?"

"No. You just said to be here at eight in the morning," Travis said.

"Oh, my goodness. I am sorry about that. It is so close to the weekend that I must have just thought you'd know I meant Monday. So sorry about that."

Travis felt a bit of relief. For once someone else had made a mistake on the job front. "Oh, okay. Well, can I at least take a look around at the place while I am here?"

"Yeah, hold on a second." Melanie opened the door to her office and set her purse and keys down. Then she came back out. "We can make the best of everything now. I can go ahead and get your information uploaded into the system and have you fill out the forms you would normally have filled out on Monday. That way you will be one less person I have to do out of the fourteen other people who will be in the training class with you."

"Great," Travis said. "All is not lost."

Melanie took Travis's social security card and ID and gave him papers to fill out. Travis filled them all out and gave them back to her. She reviewed the benefits

package with him, which included his sick time information, potential for vacation leave, health insurance,
and dental insurance. She reconfirmed that he would
be making two dollars more per hour than he originally
thought he'd be making. And another bonus that he
hadn't realized was that as an employee of Escape Inns,
he would get a discount to stay at any of their hotels all
over the world.

Once she finished going over all of the pertinent information, Melanie walked Travis to one of the training
rooms. "I want to go ahead and introduce you to Kevin.
He'll be your instructor for the next two weeks," Melanie said to Travis.

"Hey, Kevin," Melanie said to a man who was checking the computers in the training room.

Kevin turned around. "Hey, Melanie, what's up?"

"Kevin, this is Travis Highgate. He'll be in your training class starting on Monday," Melanie said.

Kevin extended his hand to shake with Travis. Travis
shook Kevin's hand. Kevin had a strong, firm handshake. "Travis Highgate. Yeah, I remember that name.
It's good to meet you."

"Nice to meet you too, Kevin," Travis said.

Kevin looked from Melanie to Travis for some expla-
nation as to why Travis was there.

"Travis is here a day early because of some miscom-
munication from me about his start date," Melanie
said.

Travis spoke up. "I wouldn't mind seeing the center
in action to get a better feel for what I'll be doing."

"Oh, well okay. I can give you a tour of the place and
tell you more about what we'll be doing in training next
week," Kevin said.

"Great," Melanie said. "Kevin, I'll leave Travis in
your hands. Travis, I'll see you on Monday."

"Have a good weekend," Travis said.

Melanie smiled and said, "Thanks, Travis, you have a good weekend as well."

"Talk about trying to get brownie points," Kevin said.

"Huh?" Travis asked.

"I've heard of being the first one to work, but you took it to a whole other level being a day early." Kevin laughed. "Man, I'm just kidding."

Travis laughed when he realized the joke Kevin was making. "I hadn't even thought about it like that."

"Come on over here. I'll show you the computer system you all will be training on," Kevin said.

Travis followed Kevin over to the computers, where Kevin showed him a portion of the system that he would be training on that next week. Then Kevin gave Travis a tour of the call center, showing him the break rooms, the bathrooms, the outside break area, and the call center floor area where people were on the phones taking live calls.

"This section of people over here is a class that just graduated from training. They have been doing live calls for about a week now," Kevin informed Travis.

A few of the people on the phones and waiting for phone calls waved and smiled to Kevin when they saw that he was walking around on the call center floor. Kevin waved back to many of them.

When Kevin finished the tour, they ended up back in the training room. "So that is about it. Everything else we will go over on Monday," Kevin said. "Do you have any questions?"

"Thanks for taking the time to show me around. I know you are probably busy, but is there any chance that you all might have training manuals? I'd really like to do some reading," Travis said.

"You are really raring and ready to go, aren't you?" Kevin asked.

"I sure am." Travis was going to attack this position as if he were the CEO of the company. He wanted to eat, drink, and sleep as much information as he could about Escape Inns. If it was possible, he was aiming to be employee of the month in the first month. No matter what it took, Travis was going to make this job work, with no excuses. He wasn't going to give them any reason whatsoever to let him go, either. As far as he was concerned, the only way they would get rid of him was if the company folded and went bankrupt.

Kevin nodded his head. "I like your initiative. Normally we do most of our training on the computer, but we do have manuals just in case our computers malfunction for some reason, or there is a problem with the power, which has never happened since I've been here."

Kevin went to a cabinet and pulled out a black binder. He handed the binder to Travis. "You are welcome to read over it. You can have a seat at this desk over here. This is the desk I use when I am training."

"Thanks," Travis said. He took the binder and sat in the chair that Kevin indicated.

"I've got to go out on the sales floor and help with escalation calls," Kevin said. "Make yourself at home. You know where the bathroom and break rooms are if you need them."

Travis took the lunch that he'd brought with him and put it in the large refrigerator in the break room. He pulled out his thermos of grape juice and took it back to the training room with him. Then for the next three hours he sat and read through the training manual, until his stomach started growling.

He took a break, went to the break room, and ate his two sandwiches and chips. Once his thermos was empty, he filled it with water from the water fountain and drank it. Then he returned to the break room, and except for taking one bathroom break that afternoon, he stayed at the desk as if he were working a true eight-to-five job.

At five o'clock Kevin came in to turn the lights off. "Oh wow, you're still here?"

Travis looked at his watch. "Yeah, I didn't realize it was five already," Travis answered.

Kevin shook his head. "You are pretty dedicated. You must really want this job."

"I do, and I want to excel at what I do," Travis said. "I have read through much of the manual, but I sure wish I could take it home to read the rest."

"Are you serious?" Kevin asked.

"I sure am."

"Well, more power to you. Take it home. But please be sure to bring it back. Oh yeah, and please be sure not to share the company's secrets with one of those other hotel chains." Kevin laughed.

"What other hotel chains? Do any others exist other than Escape Inns?" Travis smiled and then both men laughed.

Travis rode the bus home that evening clutching the training binder in hand. He held it like it was the Holy Grail. The information in the binder could help him get to where he really wanted to be. If it took all weekend, he was going to read and reread, and digest all of its contents.

Chapter 19

That Monday morning, Travis again arrived early to work. He was the first one in his training class to arrive. Again he had packed his lunch and had eaten a hearty breakfast. He returned the training manual to Kevin and went through the motions with the class as they were learning about the call center firsthand.

Even though Travis knew pretty much everything about the center's operations, the layout, and even the system for which he would be training, he didn't let on that he knew any more than anyone else. After the orientation portion was over that morning, Travis took his seat at his training computer and applied what he'd learned in the manuals to the actual computer software.

He was glad he'd had a chance to take the entire weekend to review the materials. He had taken one break to go to church. The Lord had been too good to him over the months not to go to church and praise him. The rest of the day he'd put every bit of his mental acuity into learning about his new position. There had been small differences between the manual he'd studied for three days and the computer system. But the differences were not any that he couldn't figure out. He took notes during class and was an integral part of the class, often raising his hand to answer questions posed by Kevin.

Travis knew the answers to about 95 percent of the questions that Kevin asked. Even though he knew as much as he did, he didn't try to show off, especially when he saw so many people struggling with trying to understand it all. Whenever possible he even helped his new classmates work out problems they had with their computers.

He'd worked with people in the past who acted like they were know-it-alls and this gained those people no respect. Travis wanted the mutual respect of his peers and he wanted to be a team player. There was no way he could sit in class and act like he knew it all, trying to impress Kevin to make himself shine, at the expense of the others in the class. He sure was glad that he'd taken the time to do the amount of pre-studying he had done, because as far as he could see, by the end of the first day of training, it was already paying off.

The first week of training flew by quickly for Travis. He was glad that he had a job to work from eight to five and didn't have to work on the weekends. His work schedule allowed him to be able to take on a second job. It was during his second week of employment at Escape Inns that he also started a new night job working for a janitorial service cleaning office buildings.

The first couple of days of working two jobs had been choppy. He'd found himself getting extremely tired during the day and sluggish at night as he cleaned. So he decided to set up a schedule for himself so that he could make the most of his time. He normally made it back into the house just before nine o'clock at night. So at first he devised a nightly routine that consisted of fixing something to eat, taking a shower, reviewing his notes for his next day at the call center, and reading a scripture just before praying and going to bed. He slept hard from 11:00 P.M. to 5:30 A.M.

The Marrying Kind 167

When he awoke each morning he took the time to exercise for thirty minutes in the home gym. He found that his body felt better when he exercised in the morning. After exercising he took a shower, dressed, ate breakfast, and packed a lunch and a couple of snacks to get him through the day.

On the last day of training, Kevin pulled Travis to the side. "Travis, I'd like to speak to you at the end of the day. Please come see me then."

Travis got a bit of a sinking feeling in his stomach. He'd been on many a job where they waited until the end of the day to let a person go. And he wondered what reasons they would have to let him go. He had been one of the best people in his class by far when it came to retaining information and getting his test calls and quizzes right. Then he also wondered why Kevin would pull him to the side earlier on in the day to give him a heads-up on his termination. Travis put all negative thoughts out of his mind. He was going to continue to work hard and stop second-guessing himself to death.

That evening after everyone else in his training class had left, Travis went to see Kevin. He thought about going ahead and grabbing his backpack and lunch bag first, but wanted to get the meeting over with as quickly as possible.

When Travis approached Kevin, who was reviewing some paperwork, Kevin smiled. "Hey, Travis, great." He stood. "Could you follow me please? HR would like to speak with you."

Now Travis knew that if HR wanted to see him, then it couldn't be good at all. He followed Kevin into Melanie Shumaker's office.

"Hi, Travis and Kevin. Gentlemen, come on in and have a seat," Melanie said.

Both Travis and Kevin took a seat in Melanie's office. She shuffled through some papers until she found the one she was looking for.

"Ah here it is. Travis, I am sure you are wondering why you have been called in to the office."

"Yeah, I am." Travis started rubbing his hands together. They were starting to sweat.

"Well, Travis," Melanie said, "it has come to my attention, through Kevin here, that you have done a phenomenal job in his training class. He confided in me that you took the initiative to read over the entire training manual before you even started your first day of class, and then from there you also excelled in your training class, getting the highest scores out of everyone else in your class."

Travis smiled. It didn't sound like one of the speeches someone would make to let someone go.

"Here at Escape Inns we give recognition where recognition is due. And due to the recommendation of your trainer Kevin here, we would like to offer you a position as a trainer," Melanie said. She smiled as she made this offer.

Travis's mouth literally dropped wide open as he dropped his head. "Are you serious?"

"Yes, sir, I am."

"You think I could be a trainer?" He looked from Melanie to Kevin.

"I've watched you throughout our class. You've retained more information in two weeks than some people do in a couple of months. And I've also watched you take the time to help your coworkers to work out problems they were having with the computer system as well as just understanding the concepts of the training," Kevin said.

Kevin continued by saying, "You are here early, ready, and prepared for each class, and even though I know you know way more than you let on to your peers, you keep it all in check. You don't showboat to make yourself look better than the others. These are all wonderful qualities, and you are trainer material if I've ever seen it. And I've been a trainer for two years now," Kevin said.

"So how does the offer sound to you?" Melanie asked.

"It sounds wonderful," Travis said. "What do I need to do from here?"

"All you need to do is accept and I'll update your title with the job description. Also you'll be pleased to know that your salary will increase as well. To two more dollars per hour," Melanie said.

"Are you serious?" Travis said.

"Yes," Melanie said.

"Thank you." He looked first to Kevin and then to Melanie.

"You are welcome," Kevin said as he gave Travis a hearty pat on his back.

"Welcome to the training team," Melanie said. "Kevin will help you become more familiar with what being a trainer entails next week. We have a new training class starting on Monday. I want you to assist Kevin during the class and during down times you can also take calls in the center to continue to better familiarize yourself with taking calls. It is always good to keep your skills up in that department," Melanie said.

"Okay," Travis said, taking it all in.

"Then when the next round of trainees comes in, you'll teach your own class," Melanie added.

"That sounds absolutely great," Travis said.

"Wonderful. I'll update everything on Monday." Melanie looked at her watch. "For now, let's say we all get out of here. It is the weekend, and I don't know about you all but I am ready to enjoy these next two days off."

Travis shook both Melanie's and Kevin's hands and thanked them again. Then he retrieved his book bag from the training room and his lunch bag from the break room. That night he cleaned the offices with record speed as he had extra energy he knew was because of the great news he'd gotten from HR.

He had to thank the Lord for giving him so much favor in his life. It looked as if things were finally starting to fall into place for him on the job front. Now he needed to work on the family front.

Chapter 20

Travis stuck true to the word he'd made to himself about his life checklist. When it came to his finances, he now knew where each and every cent he spent was going; from the money he spent the few times he allowed himself to splurge and get a soda from the drink machine, to the money he spent to send the clothing he'd borrowed of Brent's to the dry cleaner.

Ever since he had decided to let Jade go ahead on her merry way, Travis had stopped wearing his friend's clothing. He had also ceased sleeping in the other man's bed. It was bad enough he'd eaten most of the man's food in the freezer, but he had to stop taking even more advantage of the guy.

Monday through Friday, Travis worked hard and on Saturday and Sunday, he rested. But he still made sure to mow the grass every other week on Saturdays. On Sundays he made sure to make it to at least one of the church services. He had pretty much ceased doing double services after he and Marla stopped speaking anyway.

He had seen Marla a couple of times, but he had only spoken to her once. At first he thought she had been avoiding him, but she dispelled that thought when she told him she'd been sick with a touch of the flu and had missed a couple of Sunday services. He took that small opportunity of speaking with her to tell her what had been weighing on his mind about the double services he'd been attending and how he wasn't the man of God she thought he was.

She surprised him by saying that she already knew about the game he had been playing. While she was at home sick with the flu Marla had viewed some of the older broadcasts of the services online. It was then that she realized that there were eight o'clock services during which Travis appeared in the congregation. When she looked at the dates she knew that on those same Sundays they had attended the second service together. And that was when she started putting two and two together.

It was at that point that she bid him a good day. Travis had no choice but to do the same and he did so with the utmost sincerity. She was a good woman and he prayed she would find her Mr. Godly and Right, someday.

One afternoon while eating his lunch on his lunch break at work, Travis got a phone call that seemed to come out of the blue. He'd almost choked on his sandwich when he saw Beryl's name on the caller display.

"Hello," Travis said.

"Hey, Travis. It's Beryl."

"Don't you think I know your voice by now?" Travis said.

"I know, but I don't talk to you that often so I just figured I'd state what would normally be obvious."

"So what's going on?" Travis asked. "How have you been? How are the boys?"

Beryl chuckled.

"What's so funny?" Travis asked.

"You're funny."

"What is that supposed to mean?"

"You don't call for weeks; then you finally call and when I call back you're Mr. Twenty Questions. It's just funny to me."

"What the heck are you talking about? I have been calling you. I've left messages and everything ever since I saw you all at the mall."

"Okay, Travis, whatever," Beryl said.

"Okay, whatever nothing," Travis said. He knew the volume of his voice was escalating, so he got up and walked outside so that others would not hear his conversation.

"You know how you like to exaggerate and embellish the truth," Beryl said. "I got one message from you yesterday and I am calling you back. I mean it hasn't been more than twenty-four hours."

Travis wondered why Beryl was lying straight through her teeth. He wondered if that new guy she was seeing was being a negative influence on her. He took a deep breath. "Look, I don't want to argue. I just want to know how the boys are doing and set up some time when I can see them, plain and simple."

"You can see the boys, Travis. No one is trying to keep you away from them. You made the decision to fall off of the face of the earth, remember," Beryl said.

For some reason he felt like Beryl was trying to bait him into an argument. He heard a click that sounded like maybe Beryl had a call on the other line.

"Hold on a second, Travis," Beryl said without waiting for him to respond. She clicked over to her other call. When she came back she said. "Okay, so when do you want to see the boys?"

"I am off on Saturdays and Sundays. So would it be possible to get them on Saturday and then I can get them back to you on Sunday?"

"Oh so you are working again now? I got the notice from the child support office that you were no longer working."

"Yes, I am working now. I have a good and steady job with good benefits," Travis said.

"How long are you going to keep this one?"

"For a very long time."

"Humph, we'll see," Beryl said. The sound of her voice dripped with sarcasm.

"Look, I am working on some things in my life right now, and that is all I am going to say about that. So what about me being able to get the boys?" Travis said. There was no use in trying to tell Beryl all the strides he'd made and was currently making. She didn't want to hear his talk; she would want to see his walk. He'd have to show her what he was doing so that she would be able to see how far he'd come and how far he intended on continuing to go.

"I don't know about that, Travis. It's been awhile since you've seen them. Jayden still gets a little clingy around other people," Beryl said.

"Other people?" Travis wondered if he had heard her right. "I am not other people, I am his father." *My son seemed to be clinging just fine to Urkel,* Travis thought.

"Yeah, a father who has not been actively in the boy's life for well over a year now," Beryl said.

"I know that, Beryl. Don't try to rub it in my face," Travis said.

Again Travis heard what sounded like Beryl's other line. She said, "Hold on again a second." And with that she clicked over to answer her other call.

Travis knew that it was about time for his break to be over.

As soon as she clicked back over he said, "Could you please stay on the phone long enough to answer my question? It seems like you are pretty popular," Travis said, referring to her double, almost back-to-back phone calls on the other line.

"That was Darrin and it doesn't matter if he calls two times or ten, I'll click over each time."

"Oh wow, homeboy's got it like that, with his Urkel-looking self."

"Really now. Are you going to resort to name calling?"

"I mean really, what is so important that the guy has got to call you twice in the time span of three minutes?" Travis asked.

"None of your business," Beryl said. "And you have no reason to call my fiancé names. He hasn't done a thing to you."

"I don't like him," Travis said.

"You don't have one valid reason not to like him," Beryl said.

"He's not your type and besides he's funny looking. That is reason enough not to like him."

"Oh, please, Travis. You don't know what my type is. Please go get a life, a hobby, a woman, something, and focus on it."

"Tried that, tried that, and tried that too," Travis said.

"Oh please," Beryl said.

Travis could just imagine her as she was probably rolling her eyes at him through the phone.

"What if I told you I tried all those things and came to the realization that you are the only woman for me?"

There was silence for a moment; then Beryl said, "You really have lost your ever-lovin' mind."

Again he heard Beryl's line click. "Hold on."

When she returned she said, "Look, I've got to go. I'll think about letting the boys stay with you this weekend. I'll let you know."

"Beryl," Travis said.

She cut him off before he could say anything else. "As for all that other stuff you were just mumbling about, forget it. I am a happy woman who has a caring and attentive man, who is seeing to all my needs." She let out a huff. "I'll call you tomorrow to let you know what I've decided."

"Beryl, don't keep me waiting. I want to see my boys," Travis said.

"I won't, Travis. Unlike you I tell the truth and keep my promises." And with that Beryl clicked the phone to end the call.

Travis had to take a moment before returning to work. Beryl was hitting below the belt. She had never been that way when they were together. He wondered if it had something to do with Darrin, the man who sounded like he was taking care of all of Beryl's needs, so much that she could be taunting and callous in the comments she made. It was as if she were a completely different woman from the one he'd been married to.

He had to shake it off and get back to work. He had to focus on work and his mission at hand. There was no way he was going to let a few choice words from Beryl deter him from his goal. When he told her he wanted her back, she had paused. He didn't think it was a pause due to a lack of words, but a pause because for a millisecond she too might have been thinking about the possibility of their being together again. If what he was thinking was true and there was a millisecond of hope, then it was better than nothing. And where there was a will, there most certainly had to be a way.

Chapter 21

True to her word, Beryl called Travis the next day. She told him she didn't feel comfortable with letting the boys stay with him all weekend. And as she started to talk about not really being comfortable with even letting the boys visit him for a couple of hours, Travis had cut Beryl off and told her that he had some money for her and the boys.

She agreed to meet with him the day after so that he could give her the money. She also agreed to talk with him more about the possibility of the boys being able to come visit him.

In addition to being able to account for where all of his money was going, Travis had been able to put money aside for Beryl for child support, put aside money for housing and a car fund, and he was even able to pay his tithes each paycheck. The budgeting was working and in the end he was in the black instead of in the red. He saw a light at the end of the tunnel. Now that he was seeing light, he knew he needed to move on through the tunnel and get his wife back. Time was running out.

Travis sat, ironically enough, on a bench in front of the Piccadilly where he'd last had lunch with Marla. Beryl had agreed to meet him at one o'clock and she was now officially ten minutes late. As the minutes ticked by he wondered if she was actually going to stand him up.

The old Beryl he knew would have been prompt, but the new Beryl had been acting pretty strange.

Finally at 1:20, Beryl came up behind him and tapped him on the shoulder. "Hey."

Travis turned around. "Oh, I thought you would be coming in the front door."

She was wearing sunglasses and a scarf over her head. "I parked on the other side of the mall," Beryl said. She continued to stand and look around as if she wanted to get their meeting over with.

"Have a seat for a second at least," Travis said.

"No." She was abrupt when she said this.

"Well okay then. I know you are in a rush and everything but at least tell me you've thought more about the boys coming to visit me."

Her cell phone rang. She pulled it out of her purse and looked at it. She let it ring three times before answering it.

"Hey, sweetheart," Beryl said. "Yeah, I was trying to get to it. You know I don't like to talk on the phone while I am driving without my hands-free device." She paused. "Yeah, I pulled over." She paused again. "Yeah, I'm at the mall." Then Beryl looked around. "I'm going to run into Belk and pick up some lipstick; then I'll be on my way home." Beryl paused again. "Yes, I'll be straight home after that." She nodded her head. "Love you too, babe. Bye." The whole while she spoke she kept the glasses on and her back to the front entrance of the mall.

Travis cocked his head. "What was that all about?"

"Are you thirsty? I am," Beryl said. She looked toward the Piccadilly Restaurant. "Why don't we get something to drink?"

Without waiting for a response from Travis, Beryl started walking to the entrance of the restaurant. Travis stood and followed her. They each got a drink and then Beryl found a seat in the back of the restaurant far from the windows.

When she sat it seemed to Travis as though she let out a sigh of relief. Finally she removed the shades and scarf. And then she looked at her watch.

"Beryl," Travis said. "Is there something you want to talk to me about?"

"Okay, the boys can come visit you. Just let me know where you want to meet me. How is next Saturday?"

"Saturday is fine. How long?"

"They can stay until Sunday," Beryl said.

Beryl's phone rang again. She looked down at it and didn't pick it up this time. She put it back in her purse.

Travis was getting more of a distinct feeling that something was going on. "Don't you need to pick that up?" he asked, fishing for an answer.

"No." Beryl stood to leave. "I'll call you back to set up a place to meet with the boys."

Travis stood too and held her arm. "Whoa, whoa. Slow down. Here." Travis handed her three envelopes.

Beryl looked at the envelopes as if they were something foreign. "What is this?"

"One is for Cameron, one is for Jayden, and the last one is for you," Travis said. He had purchased a card for each of them. And inside Beryl's card he'd written her a message and placed some money in it for her. It wasn't enough to call it full child support, but it was a start. He wanted to show her that he could be a man of his word and that he didn't need some other man taking care of his children.

"Please give the boys their cards and you can open yours later," Travis said.

"You shouldn't have done this." She stuffed the envelopes in her purse and looked around.

"What's the matter, Beryl?"

She stopped. "Nothing is wrong. Nothing really." She forced a smile.

"I know you better than that," Travis said.

"Look, Travis. Everything is fine. Now I've got to get going." She pulled away from him and walked to the front of the restaurant to exit it. As she walked she put her shades back on and the scarf over her head.

Before she could get completely out of earshot Travis yelled out, "Don't forget to pick up your lipstick."

He sat back down and sipped his Pepsi for a few more minutes. Something wasn't right. The smiling-faced Beryl he'd seen the last couple of times was now replaced with a face he'd never seen before. With him she was always angry, but that wasn't the face she was portraying just now. He couldn't quite put his finger on it but he knew something just wasn't right.

He bowed his head to pray. "Dear Lord. I am coming to you in prayer this afternoon, standing in the gap for Beryl. Lord, I don't know what is going on but there is something wrong. I can feel it. I see fear and confusion in Beryl's eyes. Please, Lord, protect Beryl and my sons. Keep them from all hurt, harm, and danger. I pray this in your son Jesus' name. Amen."

Travis got up from the table paid the bill for the two sodas he and Beryl drank and headed out of the mall. Thoughts of Beryl's actions weighed heavy on his mind. He decided to go by one of the office buildings he normally cleaned to check and see if anyone had come in earlier that day to work. Sometimes people would work on Saturdays and leave trash in the bins. He'd once gotten a complaint from someone stating that he had not cleaned the building, but the person who actually came in to work that Saturday had gotten the whole matter straight.

But it still bothered him because he didn't want another mishap like that to happen again. His night janitorial job worked perfectly with his day job and he wanted to make sure things kept working well for him.

After leaving the office building Travis stopped at the grocery store to pick up some food for the next day and upcoming week. After he confirmed that his boys would be coming that next Saturday, he'd make another trip to pick up some things they might like to eat.

On his way out of the grocery store he passed the lottery ticket machine. He contemplated buying a scratch-off but thought better of it. When he got outside he changed his mind again. He hadn't splurged any of his money in weeks, nor had he done anything for recreation for himself. So he decided to buy a couple of scratch-off tickets.

While riding on the bus he took out a coin and scratched off the numbers of each of the scratch-off tickets. First he scratched off the top numbers on each card and then he scratched off the bottom numbers, only revealing the numbers. He figured there was no reason to reveal the prize amounts, especially if he didn't win anything.

On both cards he had two numbers that matched top and bottom. He revealed the winning prize on the first card and found that he had won a whopping five dollars. At least he had gotten half his money back for the ten-dollar purchase he had made. When he scratched off the winning prize for the second card, Travis stared at it in disbelief.

Then he looked around trying to make sure no one else was watching him. When he saw that no one else on the bus was paying him any attention, he looked closely back at the card again. He had just won $15,000.

***

Travis called in to work as soon as he woke up to tell Kevin he needed the day off. When the lottery office opened he was standing in front of it. He presented his ticket, and after a couple of hours of doing paperwork and the deductions taken for taxes, back taxes, and the back child support he owed, he left the lottery office with a check for $8,945.25.

All weekend he had thought and pondered about what he could do with the money and how the money would be best spent. And, in the end, Travis knew that he needed transportation more than anything else. By his calculations he could take the $15,000 along with the money he had already put aside in his savings and he would be able to get a nice car and be able to go ahead and start paying for the auto insurance.

With a car that was paid for free and clear, he wouldn't have to worry about car payments and finance charges. That money could be funneled somewhere else, like to pay for housing as well as many of the other necessities. When he had found out that his $15,000 would be cut down he wasn't pleased, but knew that the back tax situation he'd had looming over his head and the back child support were now taken care of. He could start those two areas of his life on a clean slate.

With his check in hand he pulled out the business card that Phillip Tomlinson had given him.

Phillip answered on the first ring. "Hello, this is Phillip."

"Hi, Phillip. This is Travis Highgate."

"Travis, hey, man. How's it going?"

"Pretty good, I can't complain right now." Travis subconsciously patted the wallet in his pocket.

"Is anything wrong?" Phillip asked with concern.

"No, nothing is wrong. Quite a bit has happened since the last time you and I spoke."

"Oh really?" Phillip asked.

"Yes, and all on a positive front," Travis said. "But first and foremost, this is not just a social call."

"Oh, no?"

"Nope. I am calling because I am in the market to buy a car."

"Oh, you are? Well I am the man who can help you in that department, that's for sure."

"Great, I knew you could."

"How soon are you looking to get one and when do you want to come by to see what we have?"

"How about now?" Travis asked.

"You want to come by now and see what we have?" Phillip asked.

"Yes, literally. I want to see what you have and I want to buy a car, now."

"Wow. Okay then. Come on down. I am here all day. I am sure we can find you something."

"Great, I am on my way," Travis said. He hung up the phone and caught a bus headed over to Phillip's car dealership. The whole while he rode, he was filled with hopeful anticipation that his days of having the catch the bus would soon end.

Chapter 22

As soon as Travis stepped to the front door of the car dealership the hungry eyes of the car salesmen and ladies were on him. The salesman closest to him briskly walked over to him.

"Hi, sir. How are you doing today?" He stuck out his hand to Travis. "My name is Joe. Please let me know if I can be of any assistance to you today."

"Thanks, Joe. You can help me actually. I am looking for Mr. Phillip Tomlinson."

Joe cocked his head. "Sure, I'd be more than happy to get him for you. In the meantime, is there anything I can help you with?"

"No," Travis said and he left it at that. He turned his attention to a sleek new-looking sports car. He figured Joe probably thought he was there to make a complaint or something and by the way he was looking at the sleek new sports car that was sitting in the middle of the showroom floor, he also figured Joe might be thinking that he was missing out on a great commission.

Travis knew there was no way in the world that he could afford a car like the one he was admiring, but he didn't care. It was always nice to look around. At that point he was just thankful that the Lord had given him the means to be able to get some reliable transportation.

Phillip came out and greeted Travis with a big hug. "Hey, Travis, my man."

"Hey, Phillip. Thanks for seeing me on such short notice," Travis said.

"No problem. If I couldn't have helped you at the moment, then I would have had one of my salespeople make sure you were well taken care of," Phillip said.

A few of the salespeople nodded their heads in agreement.

"Come on up to my office so we can talk about what you are looking for," Phillip said.

Travis followed Phillip up a flight of stairs into his office. The office overlooked the sales floor and the vast lot of cars in the front of the building. Travis had had no idea Phillip was such a prestigious man.

"Come on in, have a seat," Phillip said. He turned to the mini-refrigerator he had behind his desk. "Can I get you a soda or some water?"

"Some water would be great," Travis said.

Phillip pulled out two bottled waters for the both of them. Travis took his and took a couple of gulps. He was thirstier than he realized. He guessed it was probably because he had been sweating most of the morning between sitting in the lottery office, and catching the bus and walking onto the car lot.

His day thus far reminded him of the old army slogan that said, "We do more before nine A.M. than most people do all day." He had done a lot that morning and with God's grace he'd accomplish even more.

Phillip clicked the mouse on his computer to make the screensaver disappear. "Okay, tell me more about what you are looking for."

Travis had done a lot of thinking about this the previous two nights. "First and foremost I need something reliable. I would also like something good on gas. I'd like a sedan and not a coupe. I don't want to go through the hassle of having to let people in and out of my back seat.

"My pocket tells me I'll need to get something used. I mean, new would be great, but that will have to be for another day and time."

"Okay. So you want a car. And I am guessing that even though you want something used you want something with the lowest mileage I can find, right?" Phillip asked.

"Right," Travis said.

"Do you have any preference as far as color or make and model?"

"Shoot yeah. I'd like a brand-new black BMW 7 Series, but my pocket says that I can't have that right now." Travis laughed at his comment.

Phillip smiled and laughed as well. "So I hear you saying what your pocket is saying. And what is that? Are you putting anything down? Do you have a trade-in?"

"Man, I've been riding the bus ever since Beryl and I broke up," Travis said. "So definitely no trade-in."

"I am sorry to hear that," Phillip said.

"But I do have some money. And I have the faith of a mustard seed."

Phillip smiled. "Well I hear that."

Travis pulled out his wallet and pulled out the check he had just received from the lottery. "I have this." He handed Phillip the check.

"So what you are telling me is that you want to buy a car straight out?" Phillip asked.

"Yes," Travis said. "Let me be totally open with you. I know you know a lot about my history with Beryl and all, but there is a lot you don't know."

Phillip sat back in a position that told Travis that he was all ears and there to listen to him.

"You know I had problems keeping a job in the past. Not only that but I also had problems paying my bills on time when I did have a job. My credit is shot. And up until this morning I had back taxes and back child support, but now those two things are behind me.

"Phillip, I don't have a pot to cook in or a window to throw the leftovers out of. I've been living at one of my friend's, housesitting while he is abroad. In about a month I would have been homeless but thanks to the grace of God I have turned some things around." Travis took another sip of his water.

"I got a job a month ago and within two weeks I was promoted."

"Congratulations," Phillip said.

"Thank you. I started to realize that I wasn't doing what I needed to do as a man or a father. I started that new job like it was the last job on earth. They saw how committed I was and gave me a promotion."

"So you've been at this job for over a month now?"

"Yep. And that's not it," Travis added.

Phillip's eyebrows rose in anticipation of hearing what Travis had to say next.

"In addition to that job, I have also been working a job at night cleaning offices. I've been there for three weeks. I've been watching my spending, I set up a budget, and I have even been paying my tithes."

"Is this the same Travis I met back in the mountains of North Carolina a couple of years ago?"

"No, this is a new Travis. Man, I am so focused I can't see anything blurry to the left or the right of me. I've got to be accountable. I've got to be the father my sons need for me to be, and I can't do that jumping from job to job, or sitting on the couch watching old episodes of *CSI*."

"Amen to that, my brother," Phillip said.

"When I won that money on the scratch-off, I couldn't believe my eyes. And as I thought about it I knew I needed transportation. I've been spending money on the bus and taking the taxi here and there as well. All of that is getting expensive. I miss the freedom of being able to jump in the car when I want and being able to drive exactly where I want to go," Travis said.

"So you want to spend your whole check on a car?" Phillip asked.

"Yeah, man. You know it's not like eight thousand is a lot of money when you are talking about trying to buy a car, but I am just praying that it will at least get me something reliable that will allow me to get to my jobs, and to be able to take my sons to the park or museum, or, heck, to even be able to meet Beryl to pick them up."

Phillip nodded his head.

"Beryl and I haven't been on the best of terms the past few months, but here lately she has at least been talking to me. I am hoping to get the boys this weekend. It would be great to be able to put their booster seats in the back of a car that I can call mine. Otherwise I am going to have to have them trek around with me walking and catching buses."

It felt good to Travis to have a listening ear, and especially the listening ear of Phillip, who he deemed a good man of God. He hadn't been able to confide his thoughts and feelings to anyone else. He knew Phillip to be a man who would listen and give advice without steering him wrong.

"And I know I shouldn't care about it that much, but I don't want to meet Beryl at a bus stop while her fiancé looks on and sneers at my circumstances."

Phillip sat up. "Fiancé?"

"Yep, Beryl is engaged to be married. She is marrying some nerdy-looking guy. Personally there is something I really don't like about the man," Travis said.

"Travis, do you think you are possibly just a little resentful that Beryl is moving on with her life?"

Travis sat up in his seat. "In all truth, Phillip, I can't say that it doesn't hurt that she has found somebody else. But that's not the crux of it. He isn't even her type."

Phillip gave Travis a look of question.

"No, no, hear me out. I think she likes him because he has money and can and does take care of her and the kids. He is like the total opposite of how I use to be."

To this Phillip said nothing. He just sat and continued to listen, giving Travis a chance to let it all out.

"And I can't put my finger on it, but it really doesn't seem like this guy is really all that into Beryl and the boys. It is more like he has a bucket list that has a wife and kids on it. With Beryl and the boys, he has a ready-made family. Get this, the other day I saw Beryl and she was acting really funny. I mean she was walking around in shades and a scarf like she was hiding out from someone. And when her fiancé called her on her cell phone, she flat-out lied to him about where she was and what she was doing. I'm concerned."

"That doesn't sound like Beryl at all. She struck me as a pretty straight-forward woman," Phillip said.

"She is. That's the point. I don't know what is going on there. But I prayed for her and the boys right after I saw her," Travis said.

Phillip shook his head. "I hope everything is okay with Beryl. I'll pray for her and the boys tonight myself."

"Thanks," Travis said.

"Man, Travis, I must say you have come a long way. And brother to brother, I am proud of you."

It meant a lot for Phillip of all people to tell him that he was proud of him. "Thank you, I really appreciate that."

"If you need a listening ear, feel free to call me." Phillip wrote his personal cell phone number and his home phone number on the back of his business card.

Travis took the card and slipped it into his wallet.

"It sounds as if you've got things under control. We just need to find you a car now." Phillip smiled. He clicked the screen on his computer.

Phillip turned the computer screen to the side so Travis could see it. "I've typed in the specifications you want and a price range and this is what I've come up with."

Travis looked at the list of cars with their pictures. Then he looked at the price range that Phillip had typed in. "Oh, I think you punched the number in wrong. I've only got a little under nine thousand to spend. I mean I do have a little more saved but I am going to have to get car insurance."

"We've only got one car in stock that is under nine thousand." Phillip pointed to an early-model car with high miles on it.

The particular car he was pointing to wasn't a Honda or a Toyota. From past experience Travis knew that that particular brand of car wasn't very reliable. "Oh," said Travis.

"So look at the cars in this price range and don't worry, we'll work out the difference," Phillip said.

Out of the list of the other nineteen cars, Travis picked out three he wanted to test drive. He and Phillip test drove all three. The one he ended up liking the most was a five-speed automatic, desert mist metallic

Honda Accord that was seven years old. It had only 90,000 miles on it, which wasn't too bad for the age of the car. The car drove wonderfully and whoever had owned it before had kept it in pristine condition.

Not only was the car in great condition, but it was loaded. It had cruise control, a six-disc CD changer, air conditioning, air bags, remote keys, an alarm system, tinted windows, and a sunroof. The sticker price for the car was $10,578 which was $1,632.25 above Travis's budget.

"So you like this one?" Phillip asked.

"Yeah, but that price is way over what I have to spend," Travis said.

"Stay right here. I'll be right back." When Phillip returned he said, "Let me ask you a question."

"Sure."

"You say you've been trying to do right?"

"Yes," Travis said.

"And you say that you have been watching your spending and paying your tithes? Did you take any tithes out of this money?" Phillip asked.

Travis gave Phillip a sheepish look.

"The new sticker price for this car is $8,050.25," Phillip said.

"But that's like $895 below the amount of my check. That's like ten percent less," Travis said as he got the message. "Got it. Ten percent for my tithes."

Phillip pulled a sold sticker out of his pocket and placed it on the car. "Sold."

"Are you serious? That price is like $2,500 less than the sticker price that was on the car," Travis said in disbelief.

"Yes, it is. I am the owner and I can set the prices. And let me tell you one other thing that might blow your mind. The price you are paying for this car is about five thousand less than market value," Phillip said.

Travis took a step back and pinched himself. "Are you for real? I mean this is like really blowing my mind."

"It's called a favor, Travis. And the Lord blows my mind all the time too," Phillip said.

Chapter 23

Travis hit the CD changer on his new CD player in his new car. He had filled all six changers with music, ranging from gospel to R&B and jazz. He had taken that Friday afternoon off to prepare for his visit with his sons. Beryl had called him the day before to tell him that she would meet him with the boys on Saturday and that they could spend the night with him.

He had been all around the city picking up toys for the boys to play with, groceries for them all to eat, and kid movies and popcorn so they could have movie night together just as they'd had when they were all living in one home. Travis felt like he was shopping on Christmas Eve to surprise the boys the next day.

Thus far the trunk of his Accord was filled with balls and trucks for the boys to play with, plus two scooters. His plan was to make sure the boys had fun the entire weekend. He missed playing with his sons a lot.

The next morning, Beryl met Travis at one of the city parks. Beryl and her new man got out of the Lexus they were in. The car Darrin was driving had a personalized vanity plate with the emblem for Carson State University, and letters that said EXCEL. Travis also saw an insignia for a fraternity decaled in the back window of his car.

As soon as the boys saw their father they ran up to him. Travis tried to hold back tears. The boys were dressed similarly with khaki shorts and T-shirts. Cameron, the oldest, had on a shirt that read KINDERGARTEN ROCKS on the front and TRINITY PARK ELEMENTARY SCHOOL on the back. Jayden, who was three years old, had on a T-shirt that read TLC DAYCARE on the front, and the back said TENDER LOVING CARE DAYCARE CENTER with the address of the daycare.

"Hey, Travis," Beryl said.

He could have been imagining it, but it seemed as if Beryl's greeting wasn't as hateful as it normally was. It was a bit softer.

"Hello again," Darrin said.

"Hello," Travis said in an attempt to be polite. He would have been fine just ignoring the guy all together.

"They've already had breakfast," Beryl said. She noticed the tension between the two men.

"Okay. Great," Travis said.

"And, don't forget, Jayden is allergic to peanut butter," Beryl added.

"I know, Beryl," Travis replied.

Beryl pulled one of the booster seats out of the Lexus and Darrin got the other one. They handed them to Travis. He put them in the back seat of his car.

"Nice car," Beryl said.

"Thanks."

"Is it yours?" Beryl asked. Travis could hear the genuine curiosity in her voice.

"Yes, it is," Travis said. He had never owned a car free and clear in his life.

"Yeah, nice ride," Darrin said.

It was all Travis could do not to say anything back. He knew if he did, the wrong words would flow out of his mouth.

Beryl must have sensed the tension again because she quickly said, "So we'll meet you back here tomorrow at five." She pulled the boys' overnight bag out of the Lexus and handed it to Travis.

"Cameron, Jayden, come give Mommy a hug." The boys hugged their mother and she kissed them both on the forehead.

"Come on, guys. I've got a fun-filled day planned for you," Travis said to his sons.

"Yeah, Daddy, what are we going to do?" Cameron asked.

"You'll see," Travis said. "Now come on and get into your seats so we can head on out."

Beryl headed with Darrin back to the Lexus. Travis figured the happy couple would probably make the most of their time together without the kids. But as he looked at Darrin and Beryl's faces it was like looking at a tale of two cities. Darrin looked excited and relieved, while Beryl looked keyed up and worried.

As soon as they left the park, Travis drove over to the Silvermont Children's Museum. One of his coworkers had mentioned taking the kids to the museum when Travis told him that he was going to be getting his sons for the weekend. He had never in his life heard of a children's museum and wondered why in the world little kids would want to look at art paintings and sculptures. The coworker schooled Travis on what a children's museum consisted of and he was sold.

In the museum the boys played for hours. At first they played in an area that had a play fire truck and dress-up outfits. Then they played with the play ambulance that had items a real ambulance would have, like a gurney, a stethoscope, a hospital IV pole, and even lab coats. Once the boys got tired of playing doctor, they took on the roles of being veterinarians in a pet hospital. Just like the fire truck and ambulance, the pet hospital was fully equipped. The hospital had stuffed dogs and cats, an exam table, pet cages, and even X-ray sheets and an X-ray light board.

Travis had to coax them to check out other areas. There was a play kitchen, a grocery store, and diner, which all had items to make the areas look realistic. Once the boys finished shopping as if they were in a grocery store while Travis pretended he was ringing their items up on the play cash register, they headed to the three-story pirate ship to play.

They spent four hours in the museum and still did not cover it all. When Travis told them it was time to go, Jayden cried and Cameron pleaded with his father, asking for another ten minutes. Travis gave in twice to the ten-minute extension, which didn't help because the boys still were reluctant to leave.

In the end he had appealed to their stomachs. Both children were hungry. As it turned out they were also very tired. He hadn't gotten a mile down the road before both boys were asleep. Travis drove with the music off so that he could listen to their snoring. It was a sweet sound he hadn't heard in over a year.

When he got them home he fed them some spaghetti he had cooked the night before. As he remembered it, both of them loved to eat spaghetti. Things hadn't changed, they both cleaned their plates.

After giving them their baths, Travis spread out a thick blanket on the floor in the bonus room and put the DVD for the *Cars* movie in the DVD player. The boys clapped their hands when they saw which movie it was. Then Travis popped popcorn and joined his sons on the blanket for movie night. Ten minutes into the movie both children had fallen asleep again.

Travis moved them to his bed to sleep. He grabbed a pillow and blankets and made himself comfortable on the recliner in the bonus room. That night Travis slept like a newborn baby without a care in the world.

The next morning, Travis awoke early and fixed breakfast for the boys. He turned on the gospel music and hummed along with it as he scrambled eggs, made fried country ham, and poured orange juice in their glasses. He also made grits and jelly toast.

After eating breakfast, Travis got himself and the boys dressed for church. He had forgotten how long it took to get two additional people ready for church. So instead of making the eight o'clock service they went to the eleven o'clock. Even though the church had an area for children to enjoy service so they could learn at their own age level, Travis kept the boys close, knowing that in just a few hours, he was going to have to send them back with their mother. Then he didn't know how long it would be before he would get the chance to see them again.

Five o'clock came much too quickly for Travis. When he pulled up to the meeting spot, he saw where Beryl and Darrin were already waiting. When Cameron realized he was going to have to leave his father, he started to kick, scream, and cry. When Jayden saw his brother crying, he started crying as well.

It tore at Travis's heart knowing the picture was completely wrong. Travis could also see that it tore at Beryl's heart as well, as she did her best to take the booster seats back and their overnight bag without crying. She tried to soothe the boys, but it looked as if she needed soothing herself.

Darrin looked like a knot on a log. He was basically useless and void of feeling. "Come on, boys. Time to go." He sounded like a nerdy robot to Travis.

Travis held Cameron in his arms. "Cameron, it's okay. Daddy is going to see you real soon. It won't be a long time like before. I promise."

Cameron's cries turned into whimpers. "Promise, Daddy."

Travis took his thumbs to wipe the tears off of the boy's cheeks. "I promise. Isn't that right, Mommy?"

Beryl did her best to smile. "That's right. You'll see your dad soon."

"Okay, Cameron," Travis said to his son. He gave him a kiss and long hug, then placed him in his booster seat in the Lexus.

He did the same with Jayden and gave him an almost tighter hug as he knew Jayden was more confused than anything else. His cries had also subsided when the emotions of his brother and mother had subsided.

The whole while, Darrin looked on as if the whole display was a nuisance and he had better things to do. Again, Travis got bad vibes about the guy. He looked at Beryl, who was starting to get into the front passenger seat of the car. She had barely said two words directly to him. He noticed also that she hadn't made full eye contact with him, either.

"Beryl, I'll give you a call in a couple of days to talk about setting up another time for me to get the boys," Travis said.

Beryl looked at Darrin for a second first before turning her attention to Travis. "Okay," was all she said. Then she closed her passenger side door.

As they passed, Travis could see Beryl looking straight ahead with her arms crossed. Darrin seemed to be talking a mile a minute with an intense look on his face. Travis made eye contact with the guy and stared him down until Darrin finally looked away.

Travis wondered for about the hundredth time what was going on. Was there trouble in paradise? He had no idea but prayed that the Lord would look after his ex-wife and the boys. For now it was all he could really do.

Chapter 24

Travis kept hitting his alarm clock but the insistent noise wouldn't stop. Then he realized it wasn't the alarm clock at all. It was his cell phone. He glanced over at the clock and saw that it was 2:43 in the morning. Trying to catch his bearings he realized it was the wee hours of Monday. He wondered who in the world could be calling him at such an early time in the morning.

When he checked out the caller ID his heartbeat quickened. "Hello?"

"Travis," Beryl said.

"Beryl, what's up?" His voice sounded gruff.

"Can you talk?" she whispered.

"Yeah. What's wrong?"

There was silence for a moment.

"Beryl, are you still there?"

"Yeah," she continued to whisper.

Again there was silence. Travis wondered what was going on, but he was slow to speak.

"I never told you thank you for doing right by the boys. You've really changed."

"You don't have to thank me. Those are my boys and it is my responsibility. I am just sorry it took me so long to do what I was supposed to do," Travis said.

Again there was a brief silence on the other end.

"Beryl, is there something you want to tell me?"

"No, no. I just wanted to tell you that. I am sorry for waking you. Go back to sleep. Good night," Beryl said as she continued to whisper.

Travis sat up. "Beryl, Beryl." But instead of a reply, he heard a click on the other end of the line.

Travis laid his head back down on the pillow hard, wondering what in the world had just happened. For the next hour he wondered what in the world was going on. He wondered if Beryl's calling him was her way of reaching out to him, but for what?

The next few mornings the same weird sequence of events happened. Travis's cell phone would ring in the middle of the night with Beryl on the other end. Each night she talked a little more and a little longer with Travis. By the third night he'd come to expect that the phone might ring in the middle of the night.

He wanted to get to the root of whatever problem was going on, but each time he started asking questions of Beryl, she would just clam up and she would get off of the phone. So he learned to listen and let her talk and ask questions at her own comfort level. Travis could almost picture Beryl somewhere in another room whispering to him on the phone. And he wondered where Darrin was when all of her late-night calls were going on. For some reason Beryl was trying to hide her reaching out to Travis from Darrin.

On the third morning in a row that Beryl called, a Wednesday, Travis was geared and ready to listen and answer any questions she had in her normal whispering small talk pattern. Soon after Beryl's exchange started Travis sensed something different in her tone, very different than it had been in previous nights.

"Travis," Beryl said.

"Yeah," Travis said.

"I believe you now."

"What do you mean you believe me?"

"Remember when you kept telling me that you were calling me and leaving me messages, and you accused me of not returning your calls?" Beryl said.

"Yeah. What about it?" Travis asked.

"I wasn't lying. I called you when I got the messages."

"Beryl, what are you talking about?"

"I changed my billing for my cell phone and asked the cell phone company to send me a detailed bill. It showed me a number of calls that lasted for more than a few seconds from you. You must have left quite a few long messages," Beryl said.

"I'm confused. What do you mean you never got the messages?"

"I don't know. At first I thought you were lying about calling me. You know your track record with telling the truth is not that great. And you know how you like to embellish things." Beryl paused.

"I'm listening," Travis said. He sat up to give her his full attention.

"Well a couple of weeks ago I know I distinctly heard my phone ring. I was in the bedroom about to take a shower. I looked at the caller ID and saw that it was you who had called and that you had left a message. I put the phone back down without checking the message. The shower was running so I decided to check it after I got out of the shower.

"When I got out of the shower and got dressed, I thought about it and picked my phone back up to see what your message said and the message was gone."

"So maybe your phone is malfunctioning," Travis said.

"Not only was your message gone, but your name and the history of your call weren't there, either."

"Did you hit the button to erase the message and my phone call from the phone by accident?" Travis asked.

"No. I've had this phone for a while now and I've never erased anything by accident before," Beryl said. This time her voice got louder and animated.

"Okay, calm down. What are you thinking? What are you trying to say?"

"I think Darrin erased it."

Travis processed what Beryl was saying. "Why do you think Darrin erased it?" Travis wanted to be clear. Beryl wasn't the type of woman to just jump to conclusions.

"Because it isn't the first time something like this has happened causing me to second-guess myself."

"What do you mean?"

"You're not the only one who has called to say they've left me a message and I have not gotten it. So like I said, I went ahead and asked the cell phone company to send me a detailed billing sheet for the past three months and it looks as if there were calls from you as well as a couple other people that I never received," Beryl said.

"Okay, but again, why do you think Darrin erased the calls and the messages?"

At first Beryl didn't say anything. Travis patiently waited for her to speak.

"Darrin is a bit hands-on," Beryl said.

"Hands-on?" Travis sat forward in his bed. "He put his hands on you? Did he hurt you? Is that why you've been walking around cloaked in hot clothing when it is over eighty degrees outside?"

"No, no, calm down, Travis. He has never laid a hand on me," Beryl said. "You know me. I wouldn't put up with that."

Travis relaxed a little, but only slightly.

"What I mean is that Darrin wants to know what is going on at all times. He wants to know where I am, where the boys are, if someone comes to visit or if I go to visit them. With me not working it's not like I have a job to go to anymore, so I am at home a lot. If and when I do go out and spend any money, he wants to know how much, where I got it, and why I got it. So it's gotten to the point that a lot of times I do just stay home and sketch. It seems like my drawings are the only thing I have anymore," Beryl said.

Beryl loved to draw. It was one of the main things she did when Travis had been married to her. She had even had a few of her illustrations published in a children's book. Travis felt bad about not supporting her more with her artwork, but was glad that she was continuing to do it.

"And he really doesn't want me hanging around anyone but him. He has alienated my friends and even my family doesn't like to come around when he is at home. They think he is too controlling."

Travis nodded his head in agreement. "What do you think, Beryl? Do you think he is too controlling?"

"Well at first I didn't, but now I just don't know. I want to believe that he is just really attentive. I mean he knew my situation when I met him. We talked for hours and hours and he has been so supportive. Even when I lost my job a few weeks after he and I started dating, he immediately started helping me take care of all my bills. He made my car payments; I mean I don't have to ask for a thing. Then he even asked me and the boys to move in with him.

"He'd been wonderful and without a job and any prospects at home, I decided what the heck, and I moved here to Silvermont with him."

"Beryl, it sounds as if he is trying to control you completely. He doesn't want a relationship; he just wants someone he can control," Travis said.

"I think you are right, but sometimes I think that maybe I am blowing it all out of proportion."

"Can I ask you a question?" Travis asked. He didn't want her to revert to clamming up on him if he started to ask too many questions.

"Yes," Beryl said. She seemed so much more forthcoming than she had been before.

"That day I was talking to you on the phone and Darrin called you three times, does he do that often?"

"He does it all the time. That is why I am calling you in the wee hours of the morning. He sleeps pretty hard and this is the only time of night that I can get some peace and quiet to myself. I always feel like he is watching my every move," Beryl said.

"And that day I saw you at the mall with the scarf and shades on, were you hiding from him?"

"Yeah. I was trying to hide from him but somehow he still knew that I was at the mall. I hadn't told him I was going to the mall," Beryl confided.

"So how did he know you were at the mall?"

"I have no idea."

"Something isn't right. I knew there was something about that guy I didn't like," Travis said.

"Travis, you wouldn't like anybody I dated," Beryl said.

"True, but this goes beyond that. I get bad vibes when I am around him." Travis paused for a moment as he tried to gather his thoughts.

"What is his whole name?" Travis asked.

"Darrin Hobbs," Beryl said.

"Does he have a middle name?"

"Yes, it's Michael."

"How old is he?"

"He's thirty-three," Beryl said.

"Oh, so I see you got yourself a young man," Travis said, trying to make a joke. "Got tired of little old me and traded me in."

"Not funny, Travis. He is only a year younger than me and you're not that old. You're thirty-six not fifty-six." Beryl paused and let out a small breath of frustration. "Why are you asking me all these questions?"

"Don't worry about that."

"You aren't going to do anything crazy, are you?" Beryl asked.

"Beryl, honey, I may be a lot of things, but crazy is not one of them."

"Sorry," Beryl said.

"Where—" Travis was cut off by Beryl.

"Oh, my goodness, I hear something. I think he's up. I've got to go." Her whisper was so low that Travis had to strain his ears to hear her.

He spoke quickly, "If you feel at all threatened, then you get my boys and get out of there."

"Okay, I will," Beryl whispered back.

"You call me if you need me. I am here for you," Travis said.

"I will," Beryl said; then she hung up her phone.

Travis hopped out of the bed and started pacing back and forth. What could he do? Beryl sounded scared even though she was trying her best to hide just how scared she was. That guy meant Beryl no good. It sounded like he was on the fast track to making it so Beryl would be completely dependent on him, and then what?

He felt helpless as to what he could do. If Beryl had needed him right then, he would not have been able to do a thing. He had no idea where they lived. If he did he would drive over to their house and sit outside just in case Beryl did call him in need. He could just kick himself for not knowing where his little boys lived.

Feeling the need to vent out his frustrations, he went to the bonus room and started lifting weights. As he lifted them he thought about what he might be able to do the next day. First he would go to the library and do a search for the name Darrin Michael Hobbs to see how much information he could pull up on the guy.

Beryl was such an unassuming person that she probably hadn't done any background checks on the guy. Especially since it seemed like he was a knight in shining armor coming to rescue her from her circumstances. He also presented himself as a prince there to lull her into modern-day servitude.

She basically believed that all people were good until they proved themselves to be otherwise. It seemed as though Beryl was starting to see that Darrin was starting to show himself to be otherwise. From the phone calls he'd received, especially the one that night, it sounded as if Beryl was stuck between a rock and a hard place.

There was no way she would be able to do any checking on Darrin with him calling her every two minutes and continually looking over her shoulder. At least she had been savvy enough to realize that she could make phone calls in the middle of the night.

When Travis realized there was nothing else he could do for Beryl in the middle of the night, he took another shower and got back into the bed. And though he tried and tried he could not get back to sleep. He realized that although there was nothing that he could physically do right then to help his family, there was something he could do spiritually. He prayed for them.

Chapter 25

That Wednesday morning Travis called in sick to work. Luckily he was in between training classes so there wouldn't be a burden placed on Kevin or any of the other trainers to have to take up any of his slack.

He was standing in front of the doors to the library when the librarian opened the doors. He was the first one to get a pass to get on the computers. He had armed himself with a bottle of water, a sandwich that he packed in his book bag to eat later, and some money to make copies of any information he might need to print, should the need arise.

The first thing he did was to pull up a search engine on the computer and he typed in the name Darrin Michael Hobbs. This search yielded numerous people in numerous states with the same name. There were links for various pieces of information, like social networking site links, YouTube links, and links to people-search Web sites.

So to narrow down the search, he clicked on to one of the people-search sites and typed in Darrin's name and the state of North Carolina. This search yielded a list of people named Darrin Hobbs with various ages. He saw one Darrin Hobbs who was age fifty-five and next to his name was a list of relatives, one of which was another Darrin Hobbs. Travis wondered if this was the father of the Darrin he was looking for.

He reentered his search. This time he put Darrin's full name and his age along with the state of North Carolina. Immediately Darrin's full name pulled up along with his age of thirty-three, the previous cities he'd lived in, and a list of his relatives, which included his father Darrin Hobbs, and other various people with the last name Hobbs. Travis assumed the other people were his mother, maybe, and also siblings.

The site showed that there was other data available for Darrin M. Hobbs. So to see the full report for Darrin, Travis clicked the icon for a full report. When he did another window opened up, stating that for a small fee of just $49.95, Travis could get information about any property Darrin owned as well as information about judgments, aliases, if he'd been married before, or was currently married, any bankruptcies he might have had, and if he had a criminal record.

For just $2.97 he could pull up basic information like Darrin's address and phone number. Travis opted for the second option. If it came down to it, later he would pay for the full report. Travis knew that there was more than one way to get information and if he did the legwork he could find out about much of what the full report would give him instantly. He had all day.

Periodically he found himself checking his phone to make sure he didn't have any missed phone calls from Beryl. He had to inwardly chuckle to himself because just a few short months ago he was dreading a call from his ex-wife, and now he waited in anticipation to hear from her.

Travis looked on the North Carolina Department of Correction offender Web site and did a public information search. There he was prompted to put in a first and last name as well as the middle initial, the person's gender, race, and age. After inputting all of the requested information he clicked the search button.

Only one name was pulled up, and from the looks of things it was Mr. Darrin Michael Hobbs himself, with the correct age, gender, and race. He clicked on the document number corresponding to Darrin's name and Travis's eyes bugged out when he saw a record for the guy.

The record showed that Darrin had been arrested for assault on a female. For the assault, he didn't spend any time in prison, but he was put on probation. The assault had happened twelve years prior. If Travis was doing his math right, it looked as if the incident had probably happened when Darrin was in college.

So on the surface it looked as if Darrin might be a woman beater, but there was only one record for him. He wished there were more specifics as to what had happened in that case. Did Darrin have the potential to be someone who would eventually end up trying to beat Beryl, or had he just had a misunderstanding with a girl in college who decided to file charges on him? Travis didn't know. He printed out the information so he would have a hard copy of it.

Next Travis did a basic search for Darrin Hobbs in Silvermont, North Carolina. He was surprised to see a list of links related to Darrin Hobbs. It looked as if Darrin was a very popular man in Silvermont who had several accolades and various civic-club, social affiliations as well as affiliations with the Carson State University Alumni Association.

As Travis clicked on each link he saw the nerd posing in pictures with his fraternity brothers and members of the city council, and there was even a picture of him with the governor of North Carolina. It looked as if Mr.

Hobbs was a very popular person who was not only in the know but many people knew him also.

He clicked on each site and found Darrin mentioned in a favorable light. Other than the misdemeanor assault for which Darrin didn't do any time, Travis couldn't find anything else negative about the man. He looked virtually squeaky clean. Of course a lot of people looked squeaky clean until they got caught, especially the white-collar ones. And from the looks of it, Darrin was about as white-collar as they came.

Travis printed out some of the articles he found about Darrin with the various affiliations the man had. He seemed to have it all: connections, a home in a gated community, and his own business. But in all the pictures and stories Travis had reviewed about the man, there seemed to be one thing missing—a family.

It looked to Travis as if this was something that Darrin was currently working on. Beryl and the boys were a ready-made family. All Darrin had to do was slip the wedding ring on Beryl's finger, say, "I do," and sign the papers.

Then Travis wondered what Darrin's plans were for after they consummated their marriage. People normally showed their best selves during the dating stage, and their true selves after the honeymoon was over. Darrin was already showing that he was overly controlling and acted as if he couldn't trust Beryl. In Travis's mind it would only get worse.

He felt a tap on his shoulder. "Sir, your time is up for the computer."

He looked at the clock on the computer. Time had flown by. It was already noon. As if his stomach were connected to the clock on the computer, he all of a sudden felt hungry.

"Okay, sorry about that," Travis said to the librarian.
He went to the printer, paid for all of his copies, and
placed them in his book bag. Then he drove to the park
and sat at a picnic table to eat his lunch while he went
back over the information he'd gathered on the Internet.

"What to do now?" Travis said to himself. He checked
his phone again, but there weren't any missed calls or
messages from Beryl. Throwing caution to the wind, he
went ahead and dialed her cell phone number. After it
rang four times he heard the voice mail message with
Beryl's voice saying to please leave a message.

He left a quick message about setting up a time to see
the boys. The whole time he spoke he tried his best to
disguise the concern in his voice. He left the superficial
message, while wanting to yell a different message to
her voice mail. He wanted to tell her that something
wasn't right about Darrin and that she needed to leave
and just cut her losses.

After finishing his sandwich, Travis got an idea. Now
that he had Darrin's home address and now that he
had his own car, he could go over there. He wouldn't
actually go to the door, but he could do a drive by and
check it out.

With newfound energy, he threw the napkin and
sandwich bag from the sandwich he had eaten into the
trash can, and headed to his car. When he got into his
car, he only had one problem. He had no idea how to
get to Darrin's house. He didn't have a GPS, nor did he
have his trusty city map.

"Think, Travis, think," he said to himself.

There were three options. He could buy another city
map, he could go home and get his own city map, or
he could go to the local library and print off directions
straight from the library to the house. He opted for

printing off the directions at the library. Already he was doing enough guesswork trying to figure out how to help Beryl and he didn't want to contend with the hassle of trying to drive and look at streets on a city map the whole time.

According to the directions Travis printed out, Darrin's house was somewhere in the subdivision he had just entered. He marveled at the homes he was passing. They were like mini-mansions. Each home had nice sprawling lawns, and some had three- and four-car garages.

He picked up the paper he'd printed out with the directions from his passenger seat. The directions said for him to turn left on Greenleaf and then to turn right on Chamberlain Drive. He followed the directions and looked to the left for the odd-numbered homes.

As he drove down the street he whispered to himself, "One fifty-five, one fifty-seven . . . Okay, here we are, one fifty-nine Chamberlain Drive. Bingo." He didn't stop in front of the house. Instead he drove a little bit farther down the street, then turned around in one of the other driveways. A couple of houses down from Darrin's there was a home for sale. Travis pulled into the driveway all the way up to the garage and turned his car off. He didn't want to be too close to the house for fear that either Beryl or Darrin might see him.

He wished there were a way to see or know what was or wasn't going on inside the house. Questions popped into his head. Was Beryl even home? It was hard to tell since people in this neighborhood actually used their garages for their cars and not as a storage area.

Beryl was still unemployed so there was a chance she was inside but she might also be out running errands. He guessed that Darrin, who had so many hats to wear, was probably in his office or making a business deal somewhere. He wondered how long he should sit there.

His cell phone rang. And as soon as he saw the caller ID he was disappointed.

"Hello," Travis said.

"Hey, nephew," Travis's Uncle Billy said.

"Well hello, stranger," Travis said. He didn't have an ounce of sarcasm in his voice.

"I know I've been off the radar for a while. Sorry about that," Billy said.

"No problem."

"Hey, man. I need to ask you something."

"Yes, what's up?" Travis asked.

"I need for you to be my best man at my wedding."

"You two set a date?"

"Yeah, New Year's Eve."

Travis could hear the joy and excitement in his uncle's voice.

"New Year's Eve? Why New Year's Eve? That's like in two months."

"Because we wanted to start the New Year off right."

"Okay," Travis said. He closed his eyes. The lack of sleep from the night before and the dip in adrenaline was finally starting to catch up with him.

"So can you do it?" Billy asked.

"Of course I can do it. I am there for you, always," Travis said. He was honored that his uncle wanted him to be his best man.

"Great. I'll let Ashley know."

Travis laid his head back on the headrest. "Just let me know what I need to do and where I need to be."

"I knew I could count on you," Billy said.

"Hey, let me call you back a little later. I am in the middle of something right now," Travis said.

"Oh, okay. Hit me back later," Billy said.

"Will do." He hung up the phone and opened his eyes. When he looked back down toward Darrin's house, he saw movement. The garage door was closing. He wondered if he had just missed either Beryl or Darrin pulling in to it. But when he looked both ways down the street he saw Darrin's black Lexus with the unmistakable EXCEL license plate. Darrin was leaving the house.

Travis cranked his car back up and pulled out of the driveway of the home that was for sale. He figured if anyone had seen him, then maybe they would think he had actually been there to see the house.

He drove slowly down the street in the same direction Darrin had gone in. "So where are we going this fine afternoon?" Travis spoke to himself, wondering out loud.

Darrin drove through the streets of the subdivision until he hit one of the main streets where he picked up speed. Travis did the same, picking up speed to try not to lose him. When he got three car lengths away from Darrin he slowed down a bit, keeping a couple of cars in front of him.

Travis honestly didn't think that Darrin would notice him in his early-model, nondescript Honda Accord, but he was going to be careful just the same. When a light turned red, Darrin stopped and so did Travis. At that point there was one car separating Travis's from Darrin's. Travis could see Darrin through the car in front of him and it looked as if the man was on his cell phone. It made Travis wonder if he was calling Beryl to check up on her.

Darrin pulled to the side of a street and parked and Travis did the same. When Travis looked around he saw an elementary school with cars were lined up in front of it. He read the sign in front of the school that said TRINITY PARK ELEMENTARY. He remembered that Cameron went to Trinity Park Elementary. In the line of parked cars waiting for school to be dismissed, Travis saw Beryl's car.

He wondered why Darrin was at Cameron's school. It looked obvious that Beryl was there to pick Cameron up, so there was no reason for Darrin to pick him up. So he looked back and forth from Darrin's car to Beryl's car. At one point he saw Darrin pick up his cell phone to make a call. Then through Beryl's transparent windows he saw Beryl answer a call.

After a minute or so, Beryl hung up the phone and Darrin also hung his up almost simultaneously. *Maybe they are supposed to be meeting or something,* Travis thought. But his intuition told him differently. So as Darrin sat and watched Beryl, Travis sat and watched Darrin.

The bell for school rang and the cars started their succession of pulling up to the school to pick up children. Travis got a brief look at his little boy as he ran to the passenger side of the car and got in. Beryl pulled off and headed out of the school's parking lot.

Darrin cranked his car up and followed Beryl. Travis cranked his car back up and followed Darrin. While Darrin made it a point to stay at least one car length behind Beryl, Travis did the same, keeping his eye on Darrin. He was starting to get the feeling that there wasn't any need to worry about trying to follow Beryl himself, because Darrin was already doing that. If he kept up with Darrin's distinctive Lexus, then Beryl wouldn't be too far ahead.

The fact that Darrin hadn't gotten out of his car or blown and waved to Beryl to let her know that he was waiting near the school made Travis think that Beryl had no idea he was following her. That coupled with the fact that Darrin was tailing her and making it a point to stay out of sight.

Within a few minutes, Darrin again pulled over on a side street and parked. This time Travis saw Beryl pulled up to a daycare center. The colorful sign in front of the building with pictures of cartoon-drawn children said TENDER LOVING CARE. It was Jayden's daycare center.

Beryl and Cameron got out of the car and walked toward the building. Just before getting to the front door of the center, Beryl stopped and pulled out her cell phone to answer it. Travis looked over toward Darrin's car. Again it looked like the man was talking on his cell phone and again after a minute Beryl hung up and Darrin did also.

Travis was getting a very bad feeling. Why in the world would this man be following Beryl? And why was he calling to check up on her when he could clearly see her from where he was parked? It might be worse than Beryl was thinking. Not only was this man trying to control Beryl and all of her actions, he was also stalking her.

Travis followed Darrin as Darrin in turn followed Beryl. Beryl continued to run errands, stopping to fill her car with gas and then making a trip to the grocery store. After all of Beryl's errands were complete, Travis followed Darrin and Beryl back to the house on Chamberlain Drive. While Beryl remotely opened the garage to pull into it, Darrin slowed down before getting too close the house. The man pulled over to the side of the street to watch and see that Beryl made it completely inside.

Once the garage door was closed, Darrin pulled off again, driving back out of the subdivision. Travis followed him. As he drove, Travis had to wonder if Beryl actually had an inkling that Darrin had been following her around. It wasn't like Darrin's car was inconspicuous. Travis had been following Darrin for a couple of hours and it didn't look as if the guy had a clue that he was being followed. But then again, what sane person would think that they were being followed all day by somebody?

Darrin pulled into the parking lot of a business building. The signage out front listed several businesses that were in the building. One of the businesses was called Excel Investing, Inc. Travis made the connection in his mind between Darrin's license plate, which read EXCEL, and the name of the office. Darrin got out of his Lexus, locked it, and entered the building.

Travis sat in his car, trying to figure out exactly what to do with all he had learned that day. He had learned many things. He now knew where Darrin lived and worked. He also knew that Darrin had a criminal record, and that Darrin was controlling and liked to stalk Beryl, in addition to being a nerdy-looking freak.

He had to talk to Beryl and let her know what was going on. He called her cell phone hoping she would pick up since she was home without Darrin. The phone rang and rang. "Come on, Beryl, pick up." The phone went to voice mail. He didn't leave a message. For a moment he thought about going over to the house, but had no idea when stalker Darrin would show up at his own home.

After an hour of sitting in his car and watching the building, Darrin finally emerged back out. Travis followed him straight to his home again and watched as the man pulled into his garage and closed it. He then wondered what was happening behind the closed doors.

Again, for what felt like the twentieth time that week, Travis sent a prayer up to the Lord. "Dear Lord and my Heavenly Father. Lord, Jesus, I come to you as humbly as I know how with the utmost sincerity. Lord, I need for you to continue to protect Beryl and my boys. There is an evil going on and it is threatening to consume them. But, Lord, I am pleading the blood of Jesus for their protection and I stand on your Word, knowing that no weapons formed against me, Beryl, or my sons will prosper.

"Lord, please guide me in what I should do to get my family out of the devourer's hands. He means them no good. Lord, I pray you will give me the strength to do what I need to do, and the wisdom and knowledge to handle this situation and lead my family to safety. I thank you, Lord, in advance for your covering and continuing protection. Thank you, Lord. Amen."

With reluctance Travis pulled away from the curb and drove back home.

Chapter 26

Travis tossed and turned that night, unable to sleep. When his cell phone rang, he picked it up on the first ring. "Beryl?"

"Yeah, it's me," she whispered.

"Oh, my Lord, are you okay?"

"Yeah, why? What's wrong, Travis?"

Travis had to keep in mind that Beryl was not privy to all the information he had learned the previous day. While she had some misgivings, they weren't concrete. He had to be careful as to what he told her and how he told it to her. The last thing he wanted was for her to freak out while Darrin was possibly lurking upstairs.

"I just wanted to make sure you were okay. You got off the phone pretty quickly last night. I called you today and left a message," Travis said.

"Yeah, I know. I've been nervous all day. I tried to do some sketching but couldn't concentrate. Every time I looked around Darrin was calling me. I got to the point that I hated to hear the phone ring."

"It was a message about setting up a time to get the boys. I didn't really want to say anything else just in case Darrin checked your messages."

"Thank you," Beryl said.

"Beryl, are you sure you are okay?"

"No, I'm not," Beryl said. "Travis, I got to thinking about the erased phone calls and my phone detail as well as a few other things that did not seem to really add up to me."

"Yeah, and . . . ?"

"Do you remember that I told you I got fired from my job?"

"Yeah," Travis said.

"I was fired because a few events that happened all within a span of a week. First I got some complaints from customers who anonymously didn't want to leave their names. All three customers were male, supposedly. Then I made a major error on a report I submitted, which cost the company over a hundred thousand dollars."

"Seriously?" Travis asked.

"Seriously. The only thing is that in all the years I worked there I've only had two complaints and they were because a customer wasn't pleased with the warranties on their products and they blamed me for it. I was justified in how I handled their calls and situations. And then all of a sudden I get three complaints in one week, from people who said I was rude to them. They said my name specifically. I was floored to say the least," Beryl said.

"I bet you were," Travis said.

"And I know the numbers on my report were right when I did it. I checked and rechecked all of my information. But the copy that I submitted to my boss had a comma out of place when it came to order history, which caused purchasing to order way more product than we needed."

"Wow, over a hundred thousand dollars worth?" Travis said in disbelief.

"Yeah. I honestly don't know why a red flag wasn't sent up somewhere before the order went through. But anyway, that's beside the point. I know my numbers were right when I did the report. I worked on it at work and even took it home to run the numbers again. By the time I went to sleep that night I could probably recite the information contained in the report almost verbatim, and I know my numbers were right." Beryl said.

"So what are you saying?"

"Someone changed the numbers on the report," Beryl said.

"Do you think so?" Travis asked in disbelief as he wondered why someone might do that.

"Yes, and I am pretty sure I know who it was," Beryl said.

"Who?" Travis was curious to know.

"Darrin."

"Darrin?" Travis asked. He got a sinking feeling in his gut.

"Darrin was there with me that night. I had fallen asleep on the couch and he encouraged me to go ahead to bed. My computer was still on when I went to sleep. The next morning Darrin had lovingly set all of my things by the front door for me and had even fixed me some breakfast. I didn't really think anything else about it until just recently," Beryl said.

"Are you serious?" Travis asked in disbelief.

"I am. And I know I can't prove it, but I really think he sabotaged my report. A mistake like that was sure to get me fired. And now . . ." Her voice trailed off.

"And now he has come in to save the day for you. He's moved you up here to Silvermont and is taking care of your every need," Travis said.

"I am beginning to think I was set up," Beryl realized.

"Me too," Travis agreed.

"But why?" Beryl said. "And why me?"

Travis had some ideas, but again didn't want to get Beryl too riled up. "Beryl, do you trust me?"

"Huh?"

"I mean do you really trust me, when it comes down to it? Do you know that I would never intentionally do you or the boys any harm?"

"Yes, Travis."

Travis thought about it. It was Friday and if they didn't act today they'd have to wait until Monday to activate the plan that was quickly starting to form in his head. "I am going to tell you something and I want you to just trust me. Don't ask too many questions, just trust me. I'll explain everything else later."

"Okay," Beryl said. He could tell she was resigned to the thought.

"Tomorrow, as soon as Darrin leaves the house, I want you to gather any and everything that is important to you and put it in the trunk of your car. Important papers, mementos, and things like that. Not everything will fit. You are going to have to leave most of your things behind," Travis said.

"Huh, what? What do you mean? What are you talking about?" Beryl asked.

"Trust me, Beryl. Don't ask so many questions," Travis said.

"Okay, okay," Beryl said.

"Not everything will fit, so think about all the things that will fit and stuff them in the trunk. Don't try to pack anything in plain sight in the car that Darrin will see. You got that?" Travis asked to make sure Beryl was listening to everything he was saying.

"Yes, I got it," Beryl said.

"Okay. Go about your regular routine tomorrow, picking up the boys and all, and go back home."

Beryl began to speak. "How do you know what my regular—"

Travis cut her off. "Listen, Beryl, Darrin might wake up at any time."

Beryl stopped talking to listen again.

Travis continued, "After you have been home for about twenty minutes I want you to call Darrin at work. Not on his cell phone. Call him at work to make sure he is there. Ask him something you would normally ask him. The main thing is to make sure he is actually at work."

"Okay," Beryl said.

"Once you have confirmed he is at work, then you put the boys in the car and you leave and take them out of there. Drive to 122 Sycamore Street; it is where I live. There will be a key under the front doormat. Get the key. Open the door and the garage from the inside and park your car in there and close the garage back down."

"But Travis—"

Travis cut her off again. "Beryl, did you get all that?"

"Yeah, pack in the morning, go about my regular routine, make sure Darrin is at work, and leave."

"Yes, leave and go straight to 122 Sycamore Street. There will be a key for you. And then wait for me until I get there," Travis said.

"Darrin will have a fit if he comes home and doesn't find us there," Beryl said.

"Beryl, do you hear yourself? Why would Darrin have a fit?"

"Because he . . . he . . . he just would. He wants to know where I am at all times," Beryl said.

"Do not, under any circumstance, call him after you have pulled out of that driveway or answer any of his calls."

"I don't know, Travis," Beryl said.

"Well I do know, Beryl."

"What if Darrin—"

"Don't worry about Darrin. I will take care of him. Please just trust me on this. Can you do that for me?" Travis asked.

"Yes, I can do that," Beryl replied. Travis could hear what sounded like relief in Beryl's voice.

"Okay, good. Now go ahead and go back to bed before Darrin wakes up. I'll see you tomorrow evening."

"Okay," Beryl said.

"And, Beryl, if anything goes wrong, call me."

"I will. Bye," Beryl said.

"Bye, Beryl," Travis said.

Chapter 27

On Friday, October 28, Travis went to work early as he always did. He was glad that they were in between training classes, because he didn't know how well he would have been able to give his full attention to a class of eager learners. As soon as he had gotten to work he let Kevin know that he needed to get off a little early.

After getting off the phone the night before with Beryl, Travis thought about what he would do that next day. He'd come up with a plan. If his plan went well, by nightfall both he and Beryl would be able to breathe and sleep a lot easier.

All the way up until he left work at three o'clock, Travis hoped he wouldn't get a call from Beryl saying that she had changed her mind or that something had gone wrong. The one time his cell phone had rung, it had ended up being a telemarketer calling to ask him survey questions. He'd told the guy that he was at work and to please take his name off of the telemarketing list.

By 3:03, he was pulling out of the parking lot of his job. By 3:25 he was pulling up to the same place he'd pulled up to the day before in front of Cameron's school. He didn't see any sign of Darrin, but he did see Beryl sitting in the car pool line waiting for school to be let out. He wondered if Darrin was somewhere else lurking or if he only picked certain days to follow Beryl around.

When Beryl left the school she went straight to pick Jayden up from daycare. This time he did actually see Darrin parked on a side street as he drove by him. Travis had ended up driving on past him in hopes that Darrin hadn't recognized his car. But he figured with the tinted windows he had and Darrin's pompous attitude, he wouldn't notice someone like him in his ordinary car.

After picking up Jayden, Beryl stopped by a Walgreens store. She stayed in there for a few minutes; then she headed home. Just as he had done the previous day, Darrin followed Beryl all the way home, then continued driving and went to his office.

If the plan went right on Beryl's end, then she would be leaving the house in a few minutes. Now Travis had to commence with the other part of the plan. Travis sat outside of Darrin's office building and waited fifteen minutes before getting out of his car.

He stepped into the foyer of the office building and looked at the information sign that listed all of the businesses housed in the building. Travis found what he was looking for, which read Excel Investing, Inc. It was on the second floor, in suite 208. Travis stepped into the elevator. As he pushed the button for the second floor, he took a deep breath. His heart was beating like crazy. The last time he was this pumped up and nervous was when he and his teammates stepped onto the field his senior year and competed for the football state championship for the 2A division. That day the state championship had been on the line. Today his family's life was on the line.

As soon as Travis stepped off the elevator, suite 208 was right in front of him. He stepped into the door of the office and was greeted by the receptionist.

"Hi, sir. How can I help you?" the woman said.

"Yes, I am here to see Mr. Hobbs."

"Oh," the woman said. She looked down at a calendar. "Do you have an appointment?"

"No, I don't. And Mr. Hobbs isn't expecting me, but I am here to see him about a very urgent matter."

"Oh, okay. Let me see if he'll be able to see you. What is your name?"

"Mr. Highgate."

"Okay, Mr. Highgate, please have a seat and I'll check for you."

Travis took a seat in the waiting area. The office was nice, filled with high-end furniture, abstract art, and piped-in parlor music. It looked as if Darrin really had it going on—on the outside, that is. But on the inside, Travis knew the brother just wasn't right.

He sat and waited almost ten minutes when he stood up to ask the receptionist what was going on. As he did he saw Darrin strolling down the hall toward the waiting area. He was looking at some papers in his hand as if they were important.

"Ah, Travis. How can I help you?" Darrin's question sounded snide. There was a cockiness and arrogance in Darrin's voice and demeanor that Travis didn't like one bit.

"I need to talk to you, Darrin," Travis said. Darrin had chosen to call Travis by his first name so he in turn did the same. If Darrin wasn't going to give him the common courtesy of speaking to him in a professional manner, then he wouldn't either.

"Normally I don't see people without an appointment. My receptionist can set one up for you if you'd like," Darrin said. His voice dripped with condescension.

"Well I think you'll want to make an exception for me." Travis looked over at the receptionist. "You can write me in as a walk-in."

When he looked back at Darrin, he could have sworn he saw the man sneer for a millisecond at the receptionist.

"Really, Mr. Highgate, I have some business matters. I need to attend to. This is very inconvenient for me," Darrin said.

"Oh, it's Mr. Highgate now? Make up your mind," Travis said.

"Excuse me?" Darrin asked.

"Look, I know what kind of business you attend to; and, believe me, I am not here for your convenience."

Travis noticed a couple of Darrin's other employees look out of their offices into the hall to see what was going on. And Darrin noticed it too.

"We can talk out here, or we can talk in your office, it's up to you. But believe me, we will talk," Travis said.

Darrin looked around as a couple more of his employees poked their heads out of their offices. Although the receptionist wasn't looking directly at them, Travis knew she was taking in every word. He also knew that whenever he and Darrin were out of earshot they would be talking about the altercation their boss was having with a client.

Darrin turned his attention to the receptionist. "Amanda, hold all my calls." Then he turned his attention back to Travis. "Right this way, Mr. Highgate." He gestured for Travis to walk in front of him.

"No, you first," Travis said. He had no intention of getting stabbed in the back while walking down the hall.

Travis followed Darrin into the office. Once both men were inside, Darrin closed the door with a little more force than Travis thought necessary.

Darrin walked behind his desk and stood. Travis took a seat in one of the client chairs.

"Travis, I really don't know what I can help you with here. We help people with investments. If you want to open up a savings or checking account, you'll need to go to a local bank."

Darrin's snide remark hadn't escaped Travis. There was no doubt Beryl had told him about their financial situation during their marriage. If she did then she would have also told him that Travis didn't have a savings or checking account in good standing. But that was then and this was now. It all was irrelevant because Travis wasn't there to talk about his finances with the man anyway. He wasn't going to let Darrin get under his skin, either.

Darrin sat down in his office chair. "You probably don't have an investment portfolio. So if you don't have any investments, then I really don't see why you are here. I can't help you." He sat back in the chair.

Travis sat up. "I've got stock in BCJ. I'll bet you don't know anything about that."

"BCJ, what kind of stock is that? Must be some kind of petty stock in some little company that no one has ever heard of." Darrin laughed.

"No, it is a family stock. Beryl, Cameron, and Jayden stock. I've been investing in them for years," Travis said.

Darrin laughed again. Travis didn't see a thing that was funny.

"That's funny because that's not what I heard. I heard you wanted part of your stock to take care of you. You haven't been taking care of your family." Darrin shook his head. "Man, you're a joke. Coming in here like you've really got something that's worth hearing." Darrin looked at his watch. "Stop wasting my time."

"I knew I didn't like you from the first time I saw you," Travis said.

Darrin picked a piece of imaginary lint off of his dress shirt sleeve and then wiped his sleeve off. "I can't help what you like and don't like. But I know what Beryl likes. All the things you can't give her."

"You don't really care about Beryl. And you don't really care about my two boys. All you want is a ready-made family, like they will complete the happy little American dream you've got going on," Travis said.

"Again, like I said, Beryl likes it and that is all that matters."

Travis looked at his own watch. "Look, just like you, I don't have a lot of time to waste either. Wasting time is not a hobby of mine."

"Like you really have somewhere you need to go. To watch a movie, huh?" Darrin smirked.

"No, I have to go to work," Travis said.

Darrin clapped his hands. "Well congratulations, Travis." Darrin looked around as if looking for something. "I wish I had a bottle of champagne or something to celebrate this momentous occasion. How long are you going to keep this job?"

"Not that it is one bit of your business, but I have two jobs. I work hard every day," Travis said.

"Again, congratulations." Darrin's voice was full of sarcasm. "Well don't let me hold you." Darrin stood. "I'd like to say it was a pleasure speaking with you but it wasn't."

Travis continued to sit as Darrin walked to his office door.

"Oh yeah, and, Travis, don't you ever come to my place of business again with this nonsense of yours." Darrin opened the door so Travis could leave.

Travis didn't move. "You might wanna close that door back. That is unless you want to give all your employees more to talk about. I'm not finished talking to you."

Darrin took Travis's advice and closed the door. He then walked over to the window in his office. "You know, Travis, you are like a pesky little gnat that just won't go away."

"Bzzzz, bzzzzz," Travis said.

Darrin picked up the phone on his desk. "Travis, you have one minute to get out of my office or I am calling security."

"Hang the phone up, Darrin. Give me five minutes and I'll be out of your way."

Darrin hung the phone back up. Travis figured the man didn't want his employees to see him as anything other than Mr. Perfect.

"I came here to tell you to leave Beryl and my boys alone," Travis said.

"Okay, get out. I'm not leaving Beryl alone. Beryl wants me. She doesn't want you anymore. It is just that plain and simple so give it up, Travis," Darrin said.

"She won't like you when I tell her you've been following her around almost every day, watching her every move and the boys' every move," Travis said.

Darrin cocked his head and stared at Travis.

"And I'd bet she'd love to hear about your criminal history of abusing women," Travis gloated.

Travis could tell he'd hit some sore spots with Darrin. Darrin narrowed his eyes and looked at Travis in disbelief.

"And oh, I just bet she would love to hear how you set her up for the fall at work and got her fired, with your fake complaint calls and the report you altered."

"Who in the . . . How in the . . ." Darrin was at a loss for words.

"Do you know the thing about gnats? Gnats can be everywhere. They can get into the smallest of places and find out many things. And you're right; they can be very pesky as well."

"Have you been following me around?" Darrin asked.

"Who's following who, huh?"

Even though Travis had only seen Darrin follow Beryl for two days, he figured the man had been doing it for a while, and it seemed as though his bluff was working.

"How do you think Beryl is going to react when she hears all of this?"

"She won't believe you."

Now Darrin was fishing for information, so Travis gave it to him.

"Oh, I've got proof, especially pictures with dates and timestamps of you following Beryl around. And it's not like there is more than one person driving around here in a black Lexus with plates that say EXCEL."

"I can't believe you—"

"Again, I don't have a lot of time. I promised I'd be out of here in five minutes." Travis stood. "Listen to me and listen to me well. Leave Beryl and my boys alone. Do not bother them or call them or try to see them. As a matter of fact, just forget that you ever knew them," Travis said.

"Yeah, right, I hear you," Darrin said.

"You'd better be hearing me because if I see or hear otherwise, I will put all of your business on blast. I'll tell your brothers in your fraternity and I'll tell the people at Carson State University who gave you that civic award last year about how you like to stalk women in your free time. And I'll tell anyone who works for you and anyone else who will listen. Social networking is a great way to contact thousands of people and I'll even purchase that billboard across the street if I need to."

Darrin slammed his fist on the desk. "You do that and I'll sue you for slander and defamation of character."

"You can't sue me for telling the truth, and hey, if you do, so what? Like you've said before, I've got nothing to lose." Travis folded his arms. "Just think of how bad you will look. And think of how many customers you will lose."

Travis could tell that Darrin was taking all of what he was saying into consideration.

"Do yourself a huge favor. Follow my advice and leave Beryl and the boys alone. Find someone else to use to check off the wife and kids on that life list you've got, because when it comes to Beryl and the boys, they are already spoken for."

Travis put two fingers up, one at a time as if counting. "So you've got a choice, you can take the easy way out and follow my directions or you can take the hard way."

"Get out of my office," Darrin yelled.

"Gladly. I'll take that to mean that you are taking the easy way out."

Travis opened the door to Darrin's office, then turned around and spoke one last time to him. "Oh yeah, and, Darrin."

Darrin stared with hate-filled eyes at Travis.

"You got Beryl fired, and you got me fired. Now you are fired; you are no longer Beryl's fiancé," Travis said.

"What are you talking about?" Darrin asked the question with confusion.

Travis pretended he was wobbling and started singing the Alley the Alligator song as he walked out of the door. "Come on, kids, follow Alley. Jump and play and eat yippee."

"That was you? Man, you are crazy," Travis heard Darrin say just before the door slammed behind him.

Chapter 28

That evening Travis unlocked the front door to the house. He didn't know exactly what he would find. As he walked through the door, he reflected on the events of the evening after his confrontation with Darrin.

As soon as he was out of the parking lot of Darrin's business he checked to see if there were any messages on his phone from Beryl. There weren't any. He called her cell phone but had not gotten an answer.

Though he had wanted to drive straight home he also knew that he still had a night job to do. He went to his janitorial job, completed his duties, and then headed home. There still hadn't been any contact from Beryl. He prayed all went well and she had followed his advice, because if she hadn't he didn't know what to think about how Darrin would react when he got home to her.

From the outside he didn't see any lights on, nor did he see Beryl's car in the driveway. As he walked through the house he still didn't see any signs of his family. On the second floor he listened for any signs of life but again didn't hear anything.

When he turned the light on in his bedroom, Travis fell to his knees, releasing the breath it seemed he had been holding ever since he found out his family might be in trouble. There on the bed Beryl stirred out of sleep. Cameron and Jayden were also on the bed, sprawled out, asleep—one on each side of her. She looked up and smiled at Travis. "Hey."

For a moment he just stared at the three of them. Tears started rolling down Travis's cheeks. Beryl gingerly slipped off the bed so as to not wake the boys. She took Travis's arm and led him out of the room and down the stairs to the kitchen.

Once they were downstairs Beryl found a couple of glasses, and got them both some water to drink. They both sat on the stools at the bar. It was still a few moments before Travis was able to speak.

"Are you okay?" Travis asked.

"Yeah, we're fine."

"Good," Travis said with a sigh of relief. "Where is your car?"

"I parked it in the garage like you told me. You didn't see it?" Beryl asked.

"No. I didn't." Travis shook his head. He had completely forgotten that he'd told her to park in the garage.

"I know it sounds crazy," Beryl said. Her body shuddered as if cold. "Now I just don't know what tomorrow will bring."

"Shhhh." Travis placed his arms around Beryl to comfort her. Then after a few moments he pulled back and looked directly into her eyes. "Tomorrow is going to be fine."

"Travis, I know you are optimistic to a fault, but the truth is I am going to have to face tomorrow. Who knows what Darrin is going to do? I know he probably hit the roof not finding me home. He'll come and look for me. I just know it."

"Darrin isn't going to come to look for you. Darrin isn't going to be bothering you anymore. I can assure you of that."

Beryl put her head in her hands. "How can you say that, Travis?"

"I have taken care of Darrin. I told him not to bother you and the boys anymore and I think he got the message loud and clear."

Beryl's head popped up. "Really? When did you talk to Darrin?"

"This evening, while you were getting the boys out of the house, I paid Darrin a visit. We talked and we came to an understanding."

Beryl eyed Travis suspiciously.

"No more Darrin problems."

"Travis, how am I supposed to get by now? I don't have a job and I don't have anywhere to live. How am I supposed to live and take care of the boys?" Beryl asked.

"I've got this. You and the boys can stay here."

Beryl looked around. "Where are we, Travis? Whose house is this?"

"Well it is ours for about three more weeks; that is, until my friend Brent comes back home. I'm housesitting for him," Travis said.

"So I've got three weeks to find a place to live," Beryl said.

He took her hand. "Don't worry about that right now. I am here for you and the boys. I'll take care of you. Let me worry about getting a place to live."

Beryl sighed. "I am so tired."

"I know it's a lot to think about right now. It's late, so go ahead and get ready for bed. You and the boys can have my bed. I'll sleep in the bonus room." Travis stood and took the glass from Beryl's hand. He put both of their water glasses in the sink.

Travis took Beryl's hand. "Come on. I'll show you where the towels and washcloths are."

Visibly exhausted and tired of talking, Beryl followed Travis upstairs.

Travis pulled up to the curb at the Raleigh-Durham, North Carolina airport and immediately saw his friend Brent waiting with three suitcases. He put the car in park and got out to greet his friend.

"Hey, Brent. Welcome back," Travis said.

"Hey, Travis, man. It is good to be home," Brent replied.

The two men gave each other firm handshakes and a brotherly hug.

"Let me help you with those," Travis said as he pressed the button on his key ring to open the trunk.

Brent looked down at the car. "So this is your ride huh?"

"Yep."

"Nice," Brent said.

"Yeah, it is. Thanks," Travis said with pride in his voice.

After retrieving the luggage and putting it in the trunk, both Travis and Brent got into the car and headed back to Brent's house. When they arrived at the house and pulled up into the driveway, Brent commented on how the yard looked from the outside. "The yard looks good, man."

"Thanks. I tried to keep everything up, just the way you had it when you left," Travis said.

Travis drove the car up into the garage and then helped Brent with his luggage. Travis let Brent get settled as he finished packing his last box of belongings from the guest bedroom.

When Travis descended the stairs he saw Brent sitting on a barstool in the kitchen. The man was holding his digital camera. He looked up when he heard Travis enter the kitchen.

"Did you get some good pictures while you were abroad?" Travis asked.

"Yeah. Check these out."

Travis sat on the other barstool as Brent showed him what seemed like hundreds of pictures chronicling the man's trip starting with day one. Midway through the pictures, Travis started noticing a trend of pictures that featured not only Brent, but a pretty brunette woman who Brent referred to as Jennifer.

"So I see you and Jennifer took quite a number of pictures together," Travis said.

Brent smiled. "Yeah, we did." Then he paused, not saying anything else.

"So, ah, it looks like you might be pretty fond of her," Travis said.

"Yeah." Brent nodded his head. "I am pretty fond of her. I went on this mission trip to help people. I had no idea I'd end up finding someone."

"So you like her a lot?"

"Yeah, a whole lot. I mean like enough to make my parents happy about finally getting a daughter-in-law and maybe having some grandkids someday."

Travis was taken aback. "Really? You like her that much, huh?"

"I do."

"So, tell me more. What does she do? Where does she live?" Travis asked.

"She is a nurse and she lives in Boston, Massachusetts."

"Boston?" Travis asked.

"Massachusetts," Brent confirmed.

"So you're going to be in a long-distance relationship?" Travis said.

"Hopefully, not for long," Brent replied.

"Is she going to move here?"

"Probably not. We've discussed it and I've got less holding me here than she does holding her there. I'm flexible," Brent said.

"What about your parents?" Travis asked.

"Well, I'm sure they won't mind jumping on a plane to fly out to see me."

Travis nodded his head knowing that Brent's parents could and would easily fly out to visit Brent the same way other people would take a day trip on any given Saturday or Sunday.

Brent looked around. "You really did take good care of my place. Where did you find a place to live?"

"I haven't yet. We're booked at the Escape Inn for now," Travis said.

"We?"

"Oh, yeah. It's a long story, but the short version is that my ex-wife and kids are here in Silvermont now. And we've been sort of living together for the past couple of weeks," Travis said.

"Ah, could there be wedding bells in the future for you and the ex?"

Travis put his hands up as if in surrender. "Man, we are just trying to take things day by day. We've been living like a family for the most part. And we've even been going to church as a family again. I must admit, it's been pretty great. But we are taking it pretty slow. Like I said, it is a long story."

Brent nodded his head as he took in what Travis was saying. "So, what are you all going to do? The Escape Inn is probably going to get expensive after a while."

"I actually work at the call center for the Escape Inn so I get a discount. But I don't want my ex-wife and kids living in a hotel for much longer," Travis said.

Again, Brent nodded his head; then his face con-
torted with the look of someone contemplating a situation. "I've got a thought," Brent said.

"What's that?" Travis asked with curiosity.

"Hear me out on this before you say anything. I've
got another proposition for you."

Travis sat back in his chair and crossed his arms.
The last time Brent had made him a proposition, things
worked out for the best. Travis had been able to get
back on his own two feet. In his gut he felt like he was
going to be pleased with the proposition that Brent was
about to make. "I'm all ears," Travis said.

"Okay, guys, say good-bye to the Escape Inn," Travis
said.

"Bye, Escape Inn," Cameron and Jayden said in uni-
son.

"Bye," Beryl said.

The four of them climbed into Travis's accord.

"Next you all can say hello to our new house. So put
those blindfolds on," Travis said.

"Really, Travis? You are serious, aren't you?"

"Yep, now put on your blindfold." He looked in the
rearview mirror and saw that the boys had no problem
putting their blindfolds on.

"Daddy, Daddy, I got my blind folder on," Cameron
said.

Travis chuckled. "Blindfold, son."

"That's what I said, Daddy," Cameron said.

"Me too, me too," Jayden said.

"See, the boys are playing along with this game. So
what do you say, Mom? Don't you want to play along?"

"Oh, all right, what can it hurt, right? I mean people
don't have the opportunity for surprises every day, do
they?" Beryl said.

Travis, Beryl, and the children had been living at the Escape Inn for almost a month. With his employee discount he'd gotten the rooms for a fraction of the cost of the regular room rate. Now he had found a permanent place for them all to live. And he wanted to surprise them with their new residence.

During the time Travis had been reunited with his family, he had been able to reconnect emotionally with Beryl. He'd also had time to tell Beryl about all that he'd found out about Darrin and about what happened during his last meeting with Darrin. She had been appalled by the fact that Darrin had been stalking her. Ever since then, she frequently looked over her shoulder and paid way more attention to her surroundings.

Travis also filled her in on his current life and lifestyle. He told her about the two jobs he had been holding for months, and the debt he had gotten himself out of. He had also told her about how he now had a budget and didn't spend frivolously, and also how he didn't waste his time anymore. Travis had wanted to let her know he was striving to live as an accountable provider for his family.

"Okay, we are almost there," Travis said.

The house they were going to wasn't that far from the Escape Inn they had been living in, but Travis drove around longer than need be to throw Beryl off, making it seem like they were going somewhere far.

When they pulled up to their new place, Travis said, "We're here."

Beryl's hands went to her blindfold to take it off, but Travis stopped her. "Hold on there, young lady."

Travis got out of the car and opened the door for the boys. He let them out and held their hands as he walked around to Beryl's side of the car. He let her out and then led them all to the front door. He opened the door and led them in. The scent of vanilla wafted from the inside. Travis had lit candles earlier as he prepared their new place.

"Travis, when can I take this blindfold off?" Beryl said.

"In just a minute. I promise. Just stand right there and don't peek," Travis said. Then he left her to show the boys something. As soon as he did the boys screamed with delight.

Travis returned to Beryl. "Okay, you can take your blindfold off now."

Beryl did as she was told. She stood and looked around. Her jaw dropped wide open. "Travis. What in the world?" She did a 360-degree turn, looking at the surroundings of the home Travis had gotten for them to live in. "How in the world are you going to be able to afford this place?"

"Let me just say that I've got friends in high places."

Beryl nodded her head. "I am really starting to believe that."

He showed her around their new two-story home. Beryl continued to play along with Travis's game.

"This, my dear, is the kitchen where you can cook all my meals for me," Travis joked.

Beryl swatted him on his arm.

"And over here in this room, we can sit in front of the fireplace and drink hot cocoa when it is cold outside," Travis said.

Beryl smiled as she looked at the living room that was empty except for one thing. In the corner of the room stood a fully decorated Christmas tree, adorned with ornaments and colorful lights, which blinked intermittently. "What on earth?"

"Okay, we'll work on furniture for in here later. One thing at a time, baby," Travis said.

Beryl swatted his arm. "You've been very busy I see."

"Yes, I have." Travis knew Beryl had not wanted to spend Christmas in the Escape Inn; they had already spent their Thanksgiving at the inn. He vowed to himself that not only would his family not spend another holiday at the inn, but he'd make sure this Christmas was the best Christmas he and his family had ever had so far. It was pretty close but there were still eight more days before Christmas.

"Thank you, Travis," Beryl said. Tears welled in her eyes. "You knew I didn't want to spend another holiday in the hotel."

"I know and I told you I would work things out and I have. Just trust me," Travis said.

Beryl nodded her head. "I will."

Travis knew that Beryl's nodding of her head and saying that she would trust him went deeper than just the trust about moving the family out of the hotel. Beryl had had many trust issues with Travis and his many inconsistencies. But over the weeks since they started living together, Travis had been making strides to keep his word and try to alleviate Beryl's mistrust.

"I know I've let you and the boys down in the past but I've learned my lesson. I apologize for what I put you through. Please forgive me," Travis said.

"I do, Travis. You've shown me that you can be trusted and depended on," Beryl said. "Thank you."

"You are welcome," Travis said. It warmed Travis's heart to hear the words. He put his arms around Beryl and gave her a hug. She in turn gave him a tight hug back.

He showed her the rest of the downstairs, then took her upstairs to show her around the second floor. There he showed her two bedrooms, each with a twin bed and a single dresser. "The boys can have these rooms." And then he showed her the master bedroom. "You, my dear, can have this room."

On the floor of the master bedroom was a box spring and mattress without a bed frame. On the wall hung an oil painting of a verdant green countryside with rolling hills.

"As you can see, I am still working on the décor," Travis said.

"Where are you going to sleep?" Beryl asked.

"I've got that figured out as well." He stepped out of the master bedroom and into another room. "I'll sleep in here." This room was virtually empty as well, except for some toys in the corner of the room and a few free weights in another corner.

"You've been really busy I see," Beryl said. Travis could hear the admiration in her voice.

"I've got one more thing to show you. Come on."

Travis led the way heading back down the stairs. He opened the back French doors and stepped out onto the deck where Beryl joined him. "Look." He pointed out to the back corner of the yard.

There Cameron and Jayden were playing on a swing set Travis had purchased and had delivered there the morning before.

"You are really full of surprises today," Beryl said.

"I am, aren't I?"

"How did you work all this out? What happened to Brent? Where is all of Brent's stuff?"

"Brent has moved to Massachusetts and he took all of his stuff with him. That is, except for all this lawn furniture and the lawn mower in the shed."

They walked down the deck to the swing in the back-yard and sat down together as they watched the kids play.

"As you can see there still needs to be a lot of work done. A lot of furniture to buy," Travis said. "But it's a start, right?"

"One thing at a time," Beryl said.

Travis stood. "Let's get the rest of the stuff out of the trunk. I want to cook dinner for you and the boys," Travis said.

"Okay." Beryl turned to the boys. "Boys, we are going to get things out of the car. Don't go out of the yard."

"Okay, Mommy," Cameron said.

Travis and Beryl retrieved the things from the trunk that Beryl had accumulated since leaving Darrin. Beryl had not heard a thing from Darrin since the day she'd left him. Both she and Travis assumed that he'd probably thrown out all of the items that had been left in his home.

Later on that night Travis put out four plates on the bar. He had purchased four matching barstools with chair backs from the Goodwill store. He put food on each of their plates and poured lemonade in two glasses and two cups for them all to drink.

"Beryl, Cameron, and Jayden, dinner is ready."

The boys came running and Beryl walked in the kitchen behind them.

"Whoa, was I supposed to change for dinner also?" Beryl asked, looking down at her faded blue jeans and plain T-shirt.

"No. I just wanted to change."

Travis had put on a pair of black dress pants, a long-sleeve red dress shirt, and a matching Geoffrey Beene paisley tie.

"You are making me feel underdressed," Beryl said.

"Nonsense. Now come on in here so we can get ready to eat."

"Something sure does smell good," Beryl said. "What's for dinner?"

"Spaghetti with meatballs and red sauce, along with French bread and lemonade," Travis said.

They each helped the boys get on their stools before sitting down themselves.

"You went all out, didn't you?"

"I did and I only spent six dollars for this whole meal," Travis said.

"Six dollars? Really?"

"Yep, the grocery store had a deal. For five dollars you could get a forty-two-ounce jar of spaghetti sauce, a bag of meatballs, four pieces of French bread, and a drink. The spaghetti wasn't in the deal. So everything with tax was only six dollars."

"Wow. You really do know how to find a deal."

"I learned the hard way." Travis nodded his head. "Enough talk. Let's say grace and eat before our food gets cold."

After dinner, Travis and Beryl washed the dishes together while the boys played upstairs. When they were finished washing the dishes, Travis asked Beryl to sit back down with him at the bar.

"Have a seat," Travis said.

Beryl did as she was asked.

Travis sat also and took Beryl's hands into his. "Beryl, I don't want to let another minute go by without telling you how glad I am to have you and the boys back in my life. I count it as an enormous blessing."

Beryl smiled at Travis. "I have to say that it has been refreshing to have you back in our life also. I mean I like the new you. You've really taken life by the reins and turned so many things around that I really thought you'd never be able to. Quite honestly I had given up on you."

Travis bowed his head for a moment then looked back into Beryl's eyes. "It feels good to hear you say that you like the new me. Especially since I know that you did give up on me."

"I have to say that the past few weeks of our getting to know each other again have been wonderful. It is as if we are dating again for the first time," Beryl said. "And I like it." She smiled again.

In the days since Beryl and the boys had moved in with Travis, the couple had slowly started to get to know each other once again. They had gone on a few dates just like they had when they first met. They also did family outings together with the boys on the weekends. Each Sunday they attended church services together.

Travis had been focused on continuing to excel at his job at the call center while keeping his janitorial job at night. Beryl still had not found work, so Travis was the one who had been supporting them all. Travis had been holding it down for his family for the first time in his life.

"I am so glad to hear you say that," Travis said. He stood and said, "Boys, it's time. Come on down."

"It's time, Daddy?" Cameron yelled.

"Yes, come on down," Travis said.

Beryl's eyebrows rose in question. "Time for what?"

Travis grinned. "You'll see."

They heard the boys barreling down the steps. When they came around the corner, each boy had a rose in his hand. They stood by their father's legs as if at attention.

Travis moved closer to Beryl and stood right in front of her. He took both of her hands in his. "Beryl, I am so very thankful and blessed that God put you in my life the first time. I am even more thankful that the Lord has given me a second chance to get this whole thing right."

He took a deep breath and smiled at her. Then he bent down and got on one knee.

"Travis?" Beryl asked in question. "What are you doing?" A smile started to cover her face.

The boys followed suit and each did their best to get down on one knee and stay balanced. Both Travis and Beryl looked at them and laughed.

"Did you guys plan all this?" Beryl asked.

"Sort of," Travis said. "But at this point the boys are ad-libbing."

Beryl looked at both of her sons, who smiled up at their mom.

"You know people can go all around the world looking for something that is right under their nose. I learned over the past year that the grass is not always greener on the other side of the fence. I wanted to find a woman who was loving and also supportive, someone who would be a helpmate as well as someone who was down to earth."

Travis squeezed Beryl's hands. "I wanted a woman who could hold her own, and want to be held when the time was right. And I've also found that I value a woman with motherly instincts."

Travis dug in his pocket and pulled out a small black box. "It seems like I've been all around the world looking for what I already had in the first place."

He opened the box. "Beryl, will you marry me, again?" Travis asked.

Beryl looked at the box and the ring it held. "Travis, what in the world?"

The box contained an engagement ring. It wasn't the same ring Beryl had worn for years while married to

Travis. Travis had gone out and purchased a new ring for her.

"I wanted to get you another ring. I wanted there to be a new ring for our new beginning," Travis said.

"Travis, it is beautiful. Absolutely beautiful," Beryl said.

"So how about it? Will you marry me?"

Without hesitation Beryl said, "Yes."

Travis took the ring out of the ring box and placed it on her left ring finger. He then stood and they hugged and kissed. They didn't stop kissing until they both felt tugging on their clothing.

"Mommy, Mommy," Cameron said.

"Yes, baby?" Beryl said.

"This is for you." Cameron handed his mother his rose. Then Jayden handed his mother the rose he held.

"Thank you, boys," Beryl said. She gave each a tight hug. Beryl looked at the ring on her finger with admiration.

"I know it isn't a rock like the one Darrin offered you, but . . ."

"But nothing. Darrin is in the past. Thank the Lord I didn't end up marrying that guy with his stalking self. I hope I never have to see him again."

"If he takes heed to the talk I had with him, then he won't come anywhere near you, the kids, or me ever."

"I'm glad you were there to intervene. You had our best interest in mind," Beryl said.

"Oh yeah. There is something I forgot to tell you about," Travis said.

"What's that?"

"Remember when I told you about the conversation I had with Darrin that day I met him at his office?"

"Yeah, I remember," Beryl said.

"Well, when I was telling him to leave you alone, I also told him he was fired."

"Fired?" Beryl asked.

"Yeah. I told him that because he got you fired first and because he also got me fired, he was now fired." Travis chuckled. "You should have seen the look on his face."

Beryl chuckled. "You are too funny." Then as if thinking about what he said, she said, "What do you mean he got you fired?"

"When was the last time you had any red slushy ICEE?" Travis asked.

"Come to think about it, the last time I had one was—"

Travis cut her off saying, "At Alley's." Travis grinned and started dancing around as he sang the Alley the Alligator song. "Come on, kids, follow Alley. Jump and play and eat yippee."

Beryl's eyes grew wide. "That was you?"

Travis nodded his head. "Yep."

Beryl busted out laughing and Travis laughed along with her. They laughed until they started crying. Then the boys started laughing with them also, even though it was clear the two had no idea what they were laughing about.

Travis and Beryl hugged each other. Then the boys joined the hug by holding on to their parents' legs.

"I am such a blessed man," Travis whispered into Beryl's ear. Then he looked up toward heaven and said, "Thank you, Lord."

Discussion Questions

1. What do you think about Travis's situation in the beginning of the novel?

2. Why do you think Travis was unable to keep a steady job for so long?

3. Why do you think Travis was finally able to keep not just one but two jobs in the end?

4. What do you think about Travis's idea to become a player and to find a woman?

5. What do you think Travis's motivations were to become a player?

6. What are your thoughts on Travis's relationship with Beryl in the beginning of the novel?

7. What kind of progression did you notice throughout the novel as far as Travis's thoughts and actions?

8. Do you think that Travis will be able to continue to keep a steady job and take care of his family?

9. Do you think that in the end, Travis finally realized that the marrying kind of woman he had always been looking for was Beryl?

Discussion Questions

10. How do you feel about the way Travis handled Darrin?

11. Do you think Darrin will try to cause any more problems?

12. What are your thoughts about Darrin?

13. Do you think that Beryl now appreciates Travis for the man he is showing himself to be?

14. What was your most favorite thing about the novel?

15. What did you think about the ending of this novel?

16. Did you know that Travis and Beryl's story began in Monique Miller's previous novel titled *Redemption Lake?*

About the Author

Monique Miller is a native of North Carolina. She currently lives in the Raleigh-Durham, North Carolina area with her family. For more information about the author, you can log on to www.authormoniquemiller.com or contact her at authormoniquemiller@yahoo.com.

UC HIS GLORY BOOK CLUB!

www.uchisglorybookclub.net

UC His Glory Book Club is the spirit-inspired brain-child of Joylynn Jossel, Author and Acquisitions Editor of Urban Christian, and Kendra Norman-Bellamy, Author for Urban Christian. This is an online book club that hosts authors of Urban Christian. We welcome as members all men and women who have a passion for reading Christian-based fiction.

UC HIS GLORY BOOK CLUB pledges our commitment to provide support, positive feedback, encouragement, and a forum whereby members can openly discuss and review the literary works of Urban Christian authors.

There is no membership fee associated with UC His Glory Book Club; however, we do ask that you support the authors through purchasing, encouraging, providing book reviews, and of course, your prayers. We also ask that you respect our beliefs and follow the guidelines of the book club. We hope to receive your valuable input, opinions, and reviews that build up, rather than tear down our authors.

Urban Christian His Glory Book Club

WHAT WE BELIEVE:

—We believe that Jesus is the Christ, Son of the Living God.

—We believe the Bible is the true, living Word of God.

—We believe all Urban Christian authors should use their God-given writing abilities to honor God and share the message of the written word God has given to each of them uniquely.

—We believe in supporting Urban Christian authors in their literary endeavors by reading, purchasing and sharing their titles with our online community.

—We believe that in everything we do in our literary arena should be done in a manner that will lead to God being glorified and honored.

—We look forward to the online fellowship with you. Please visit us often at *www.uchisglorybookclub.net*.

Many Blessing to You!
Shelia E. Lipsey,
President, UC His Glory Book Club

Notes

Notes

Notes

ORDER FORM
URBAN BOOKS, LLC
78 E. Industry Ct
Deer Park, NY 11729

Name:(please print):_____

Address: _____

City/State: _____

Zip: _____

QTY	TITLES	PRICE

Shipping and handling-add $3.50 for 1st book, then $1.75 for each additional book.
Please send a check payable to:
   Urban Books, LLC
Please allow 4-6 weeks for delivery

ORDER FORM
URBAN BOOKS, LLC
78 E. Industry Ct
Deer Park, NY 11729

Name: (please print):_____

Address: _____

City/State: _____

Zip: _____

QTY	TITLES	PRICE
	3:57 A.M Timing Is Everything	$14.95
	A Man's Worth	$14.95
	A Woman's Worth	$14.95
	Abundant Rain	$14.95
	After The Feeling	$14.95
	Amaryllis	$14.95
	An Inconvenient Friend	$14.95
	Battle of Jericho	$14.95
	Be Careful What You Pray For	$14.95
	Beautiful Ugly	$14.95
	Been There Prayed That:	$14.95
	Before Redemption	14.95

Shipping and handling-add $3.50 for 1st book, then $1.75 for each additional book.

Please send a check payable to:

Urban Books, LLC

Please allow 4-6 weeks for delivery